FREE FALLING

THE POINTE HILL SERIES: BOOK ONE

G.G. WYNTER

Kingston 10
MEDIA

To my family

ACKNOWLEDGMENTS

For a solitary activity, writing a book certainly requires a lot of teamwork. Fortunately, I've had a wonderful team of friends and family with me throughout the entire process.

My deepest thanks to my parents, Monica and Dennis, and my sisters, Nicole and Jacqueline, for being my first fans and to my Aunt Lorraine for being my most vocal.

Thanks to my dear friend Pedro Ajala for his constant cheerleading throughout our decade-long friendship.

Thanks to the members of the original Saturday morning Kavarna critique group whose feedback helped *Free Falling* evolve from a short story to the novel it is today: Sarah Zureick-Brown, Tory Craig Bunce, and Kay Heath. Special thanks to Terra Weiss for her story plotting wizardry and her unwavering friendship and support.

Thanks to Roger Johns, Deb Lacativa, and Anne O'Brien Carelli for excellent advice and feedback on early drafts.

Thanks to all my friends in the Writer Unboxed community who, by way of sharing their own stories, have contributed to my ability to share mine.

Thanks to Tanya Teat Foreman, Amanda Dawson, Fran Lee, and Monica Wynter for being amazing beta readers.

Thanks to my friends on social media who have liked, commented, and offered encouragement on all my writing-related posts.

Finally, thanks to John Stockman, whose eagle eyes, red pen, and attention to detail helped put the finishing touches on *Free Falling*.

The past is never dead. It's not even past.
– William Faulkner

CHAPTER ONE

I've got five minutes, three blocks, and one chance. As I race up Turner Street, my messenger bag bumps against my thigh in time with my breathing. The swell of Friday evening commuters heading in the opposite direction slows my pace, and by the time I make it to the corner of Elm, I'm down to two minutes.

The building, halfway down the block on my left, is just six stories tall, but it juts above the neighboring storefronts like an ugly, glass-encased sore thumb. I skid to a stop in front of the building and look up. Ragged gray clouds float across the mirrored windows, and I feel as if I'm looking into the eye of a brewing storm. I yank open the door and enter the lobby anyway.

The lobby's air conditioning is on full blast, a balm against the stifling hot days of the Georgia summer. The perspiration on my T-shirt cools in an instant, causing the material to cling to my skin. A chill runs through me, and I can't tell if it's from the cold air or because I've come all this way to confront C. J. Eubanks, and I have no idea what I'm going to say to the bastard when I see him. If I get to see him at all.

"Hey there, Freedom," Sam says, smiling down at me from his security perch. Sam's the building's chief security guard and a regular at my family's restaurant. And besides my mother, he's one of the only people who calls me by my full name.

"Free," I remind him gently, waving as I try to get by him without engaging in small talk.

"Where you headed in such a hurry this late on a Friday afternoon? You know almost everyone's gone." Sam smiles, his deep dimples visible even through his salt-and-pepper beard.

As I backpedal toward the elevators my mind races to come up with a story for Sam and his truth-serum dimples. "We've got a big catering order coming up and I need to finalize a few things with the client." Technically it's not a lie. We do have a big order coming up, just not for anyone in this building. And if Sam knew this was an unscheduled visit, he'd try to call upstairs, ruining my plan to catch Eubanks off guard.

"You and Agnes are always working so hard. I guess that's why y'all have the best restaurant in Pointe Hill." He clears his throat. "How *is* Agnes by the way?" His smile widens when he asks about my mother. For once I'm grateful for Sam's interest in her, since it seems to take his mind off me going upstairs.

"She's great," I say, arriving at the elevators as one of the doors open.

"Hard-working woman, that Agnes," Sam says, mostly to himself, before returning his attention to his security monitor.

On the elevator, I press the button for the sixth floor then tuck a loose braid back into my bun. The elevator's steel panel walls distort my image, but not so much that I can't see the dusting of flour on the front of my T-shirt. I brush the flour off as best as I can, then tug at the T-shirt to remove some of the wrinkles. Maybe I should have waited. Maybe I should have given it the weekend and tried to make an appointment to see Eubanks on Monday. I contemplate pressing the "L" button to return to the lobby, but then my mom's words come to me as clearly as the music coming from the elevator's speakers. "*I don't know if we can keep going like this. I don't know if we should.*" And then, "*I'm not signing the lease, Free.*"

Eleven and a half months. She didn't even make it a year before giving up. I press the button for the sixth floor over and over, as if pressing it can stop my mother's voice from repeating in my head.

The elevator doors open across from a suite whose door is emblazoned with the CHI logo and the tagline—Chronus Holdings Incorporated: Growing Communities, Shaping Lives. "Shaping lies is more like it," I mumble as I exit the elevator and step onto carpet so plush, I sink into it as I make my way toward the door.

On the wall next to the suite's entrance is a poster featuring a mock-up of a high-end strip mall. At the center of the image are a couple of Barbie and Ken lookalikes, and judging by the expressions on their faces and the designer shopping bags in their hands, they've achieved nirvana simply by shopping. Everything, from the poster to the carpet to the rich wood paneling on the walls, confirms what I've thought about CHI since the developer's real estate signs started popping up all over town. Money, and not community, is what drives their expansion into Pointe Hill.

I march toward the doors, hoping that at five o' clock on a Friday evening the CHI gatekeeper is gone for the day, but that C. J. Eubanks is not. When I open the suite's door, I'm in luck. The chair behind the receptionist desk is empty. But my luck is short-lived. Down the hall, a group of women dressed in pencil skirts and power suits huddle together speaking softly.

I glance down at my black Converses, wipe my sweaty palms on my leggings, and try not to think about how out of place I look. I'm here for a reason, and my fashion sense, or lack of it, isn't it.

Hoping Eubanks's office is at this end of the hallway, I turn away from the group.

"Can I help you?"

At the sound of the voice, I stop mid-stride and whip around to see a woman near the reception desk with her head cocked and her hands on her hips. Her hair, up in a bun that puts mine to shame, is so glossy it looks shellacked. Her eyes take me in from head to toe before she offers a tight smile. A smile that quickly fades when I take a step back.

She drops her arms and shakes her head like a school-teacher reprimanding an unruly student. The bun doesn't budge.

I take a few more steps back, pressing my messenger bag tightly against my leg.

"Can I help you?" she repeats, louder this time and with none of the clipped politeness of her first inquiry.

We stare at each other until I turn and speed-walk down the hallway, checking the nameplates of each door I pass.

"Excuse me!" She's yelling, and now her voice sounds more MMA than MBA.

At the last door at the end of the hallway, I finally see his name. I grab the door's cold metal handle and fling it open, the Bun hot on my heels.

"You can't go in there" is the last thing I hear before I close the door behind me and lean against it to hold her off.

I turn to address the man I've just broken a few trespassing laws to confront, but instead of the cold, hard eyes of a corporate bigwig, I'm greeted by an unoccupied leather chair behind a wide, glass-topped desk. The desk is pristine, empty except for a laptop, a box of tissues, and a stack of papers held down by a large stone paperweight.

The door handle turns behind me, and I move just in time for the Bun to come stumbling in. I'm about to interrogate her about Eubanks when I hear someone clear his throat.

He's standing in the far corner of the large office looking out the floor-to-ceiling windows. He doesn't even turn to acknowledge us.

"Mr. Eubanks, I tried—" the Bun begins.

"It's okay, Melissa," he says, still facing the window.

That voice.

My body reacts before my mind has a chance to. Even though I'm still sweating from running, the hairs on my arms rise in goose bumps. I swear my heart stalls before it sputters to life again, pounding in my chest, and in my ears, and in my head.

When I hear him say, "Ms. Spalding and I are acquainted," my mind catches up with my body, and I know.

I haven't heard that voice in seven years, but I know.

"Oh my God," I say, squeezing my eyes shut. When I open them, he is behind the desk staring at me. His face looks older, the jaw wider, the green eyes impossibly greener. But it's still his face. It's Christopher Bellamy, and seven years ago he broke my heart into a million little pieces.

CHAPTER TWO

———————

The door clicks shut behind me as I stare at him.

Christopher Bellamy is back in Pointe Hill, and I didn't even warrant so much as a text.

My body is still working faster than my mind. I want to punch him *and* hug him, crumple into the chair in front of me *and* turn and run from the room. When my eyes dart to the paperweight on the desk and my fingers twitch at the thought of hurling it at his head, my mind finally takes control and sends a message to my mouth. *"You're* C. J. Eubanks?"

The boy I knew as Christopher stands behind his pristine desk in his perfectly tailored pinstripe suit with not a hair on his dark curly head out of place and watches me, his eyes unreadable, his face expressionless. He is ice.

But I'm fire, and I want to burn that blank expression off his face. I open my mouth, ready to spit flames, when he finally speaks.

"Freedom, it's good to see you."

He says this so calmly, so matter-of-factly, I glance at the paperweight again and contemplate adding an assault charge to the trespassing charges I'm probably already racking up.

"Seven years. Seven years, and a 'Freedom, it's good to see you' is the best you can do?" I clench my fists so tightly my fingernails bite into my palms. The pain reminds me why I'm there, and I reach into my bag, pull out the papers, and toss them on his desk. "And what the hell is this?"

"I thought you'd want to catch up on old times first, but we can dispense with the niceties if that's what you'd prefer. This"—he points to the papers—"is business."

"Business? Don't tell me you actually buy that bullshit company tagline about growing communities. The commercial district CHI is developing will force half the tenants in that section of the Old Sixth Ward out of business. There's no way any of us can afford a rent increase, and you know it. You want us all out so you can move new tenants in at what, double what we're currently paying?"

Christopher folds his arms across his chest. "It's business, Free. Pointe Hill needs this project. None of this is personal."

"*All* of this is personal. That restaurant was my father's whole life. Dad ran Cecelia's for twenty years. He is—was . . ." I pause, still not used to referring to my father in the past tense, "a fixture in this community. Cecelia's still is. And if you think I'm going to let you take that restaurant away from us without a fight, you've got another thing coming." I wave a hand in his direction. "The suit and tie might fool some people into thinking you're some upright businessman trying to help the community, but I know better. I fell for your lies once. I won't make that mistake again."

If the callback to our past fazes Christopher, he's an even better liar than I remember, because my comment gets nothing out of him. When he remains silent, I add, "I'm glad Dad's not here to see what you're doing."

"Mr. Spalding would have wanted—"

"Don't you *dare* tell me what my father would have wanted. You lost that right when you decided to have a hand in dismantling the thing he spent his life building."

At last his eyes reflect something other than cold disinterest. "I was sorry to hear about his passing. And I'm sorry he won't be here to experience Pointe Hill's progress. Our family's goal with this project—"

"Our?"

"CHI is my father's company," Christopher says, nodding. "We're headquartered in New York with branches in London and Atlanta. This office in Pointe Hill is the first of many satellite offices we hope to open in smaller cities around the country. Jason has been handling our properties in the southeast while I've traveled between New York and London. He recently asked for my help here."

"Wait, Jason is in Pointe Hill, too?" I ask.

Jason is Christopher's older brother. They weren't close when I knew them as teenagers, so I'm surprised Jason would ask him for help now. I'm even more surprised Christopher would give it, especially after everything that happened.

Christopher narrows his eyes. "Apparently, he's not as averse to this place as I am."

I shake my head and toss my bag on the chair in front of me. Jason's back in Pointe Hill, and I didn't know about that either.

"Jason was never great at keeping in touch," Christopher says as if reading my mind. "And I've never had a good reason to come back."

His features harden when he says this, and that look

reminds me I'm not talking to the Christopher I once knew, but to C. J. Eubanks.

"So, screwing me over once wasn't enough. You come back to finish the job? That's rich, even for you."

His skin colors under the collar of his white dress shirt, and in one fluid motion he walks over to his desk and presses the intercom. "Melissa, you can call it a night." He disconnects the call without waiting for an answer, and loosens his tie, his eyes trained on me the entire time. "You really want to go there, Free? Wanna talk about screwing people over? Then let's talk. How about we start by you telling me why, if you cared so much about me, you slept with Jason."

CHAPTER THREE

The box of tissues bounces off the side of Christopher's head and lands with a plunk onto the carpet.

"What the—?" His hand shoots up to the spot on his head where the box clipped him.

"You're lucky the paperweight was out of reach," I snap.

I glance at the paperweight, and Christopher uses one hand to move it closer to him while he rubs his head with the other.

"What did Jason tell you?" I ask.

He drops his hand from his head. His skin is pink from where the edge of the box hit him. "Jason wouldn't tell me anything about that night. He said I didn't deserve to know."

"He's right."

"So, you're not going to tell me, either?"

I want to give in, want to reveal every detail about the night he squeezed what he'd left of my heart into a pulpy mess for his brother to clean up, but I don't. I don't want Christopher to think I still care. Don't want him to think it still hurts. "Bottom line, Jason was there for me when you weren't."

Christopher pulls his loosened tie through his shirt collar and flips it onto his desk, then takes a seat. "I was eighteen, Free. There was so much more going on than you could have possibly known. We all made mistakes back then."

I lean across the desk and jab my finger at his chest. "A mistake is grabbing a diet soda when you want a regular one. It's forgetting to tell your server you want your salad dressing on the side. You and that . . ." I take a deep breath to compose myself. "You know what? It doesn't even matter anymore. You and I are ancient history, and I'm not here for a walk through the ruins."

I point to the papers on his desk. "We're . . ." I begin, hesitating because I know that saying "we" is stretching it. When I left the restaurant less than half an hour ago, my mother had already given up. I go with it anyway. "We're going to sign the lease, we just need a little more time. The freezer at the restaurant is acting up, and I'll need to replace it soon. And there are a few bills I need to get ahead of, but I've got a couple really promising catering gigs in the pipeline."

I look around the office before returning my attention to him. The office, the suit, the slick hair, all belong to a Christopher I barely recognize. But *those eyes*. When he leans back in his chair and looks up at me, I finally get a glimpse of the Christopher I remember. The pre-heart-break, pre-corporate Christopher. It gives me just enough hope to ask him for help. "Look, I didn't know what would happen when I got here today. I didn't know you were the man I'd be meeting. I just knew I had to try and save the restaurant." I rest my hands on his desk and lean forward.

"So it's just you and me now, and regardless of what happened between us in the past, my father was good to you. His memory deserves better than this. If you could just . . ."

Christopher looks down at his watch, a watch that could probably pay the rent on Cecelia's for the next few months. When he looks up, he stares past me, stone-faced. Ice.

I step back, then say the words I know will thaw him. "When your own father didn't give a damn about you, mine did. When you didn't know if you had food at your house, he sent you home with food from the restaurant. And *your* father? Before he showed up that summer of our junior year, you didn't even know who he was."

The ice cracks, an almost audible snap that, for a split second, makes Christopher look shaky. But he recovers quickly. "Yet this," he says, standing and surveying his office, his arms spread wide, "will be my father's legacy to me." He takes me in slowly, from the top of my disheveled bun to my road-weary Converses. He glares at the papers on his desk and points at them. "And that *mess* is what your father left you."

The blow lands where it hurts most. Right to my pride. Right to the spot he left raw so many years ago. But I don't react to his words; I don't even flinch. Instead, I grab a pen from my bag, drag the lease agreement toward me, and flip to the last page. "I don't need your favors, and I don't need your help. I don't now, and I didn't back then." My hand shakes as I sign the line above the word *Lessee*. I'll beg Mom for forgiveness later.

Christopher and I stare at each other. The whir of the air conditioner kicks in as we stand inches from each other and miles away from the kids we were when we first fell in love. I'm halfway to the door before it dawns on me that I haven't asked the question I wanted to ask the minute I realized he was C. J. Eubanks.

"Why did you change your name?" I ask, looking over my shoulder at him.

He pauses as if weighing whether or not to answer. "Eubanks is my father's last name."

I nod, letting out as derisive a laugh as I can muster.

"What?" he snaps.

"Before you met him, before you knew what kind of man he really was, you used to say you wanted to be just like your father. Well congratulations, Christopher, now you are."

A twitch in his jaw is the only sign that my words affect him. I throw the door open and head down the hall, past the Bun—who obviously didn't heed her boss's order to leave—through the glass-windowed doors, and across carpet that now feels as heavy as quicksand under my feet.

"Aargh!" I kick the cement base of the bus stop bench. The woman sitting on the bench—who's been ignoring me since I stalked up to the bus stop—shoots me a dirty look.

"Sorry," I mumble, apologizing to both her and my throbbing foot. I hobble around to where she's sitting. "What time does the 5:15 bus usually get here?"

The old woman pulls her sweater up on her shoulders and without a trace of humor, says, "5:15."

I bite my lip and count to ten. My mouth has already done enough damage for the day. Besides, neither the woman nor the bench have anything to do with how I'm feeling. This is all about Christopher. He and I were inseparable during our sophomore and junior years in high school. When we weren't at school, we were at Cecelia's. I can't believe he's been back in Pointe Hill and didn't tell me. I can't believe he called Cecelia's a mess. And I can't believe I still care.

By the time the bus arrives, the air around me is charged with the electricity of an incoming storm and the current of my own anger. The bus is packed with a mix of Friday evening commuters and students eager to start the weekend. There are no available seats, so I stand by the back door and press my forehead against the cool window just as the plinking of raindrops begin on the bus's metal roof.

Christopher is back in Pointe Hill.

I close my eyes. It's not that I never imagined seeing him again. Hell, I've written, directed, and starred in that scene a thousand times. Christopher would see me across a crowded room, and his jaw would drop. I would be sharp, sophisticated, and successful. I would be the Laura Winslow to his Steve Urkel, the Penny to his Leonard. What I would *not* be was wearing an old T-shirt over a sports bra that made my boobs look like a caged pool noodle.

My phone buzzes and I grab it, checking the screen before answering. "Hey, cuz."

"Where are you?" my cousin, Iris, asks.

"On my way home."

"I guess things didn't go too well with Eubanks."

I roll my eyes. "How long did it take before your BFF called you to snitch on me?"

My mother and her only niece are close. Even more so since Dad's death a little less than a year ago. It bugs me when Mom confides in Iris, and then I feel guilty about it. And that bugs me, too.

"Your mother is just worried about you. The way she

tells it, you stormed out of the restaurant like a bat out of, well, she didn't say *hell*, but she wanted to."

"I had to do something. *She* sure wasn't going to. Anyway, Simone's still coming by the restaurant tomorrow for the tasting, right?"

Simone is Iris's new boss at Solstice, the event management company where Iris works. A few weeks ago, Iris arranged it so that Cecelia's would get the catering contract for a few of Solstice's smaller events. Everything had been "cook and curry," as my mother would say. Or it had been until Simone took over day-to-day management of the firm.

Iris grunts. "She'll be there. I still can't believe Garrett is retiring. Simone might be his daughter, but event planning sure isn't in her DNA. She couldn't plan a successful U-turn. But he's determined to hand over the reins of his company to her, so—"

"But we *are* going to get the gig, right?"

"Simone coming tomorrow is a formality. Garrett loves you. Anyway, it's bad enough I have to talk *to* her when I'm in the office. I don't want to talk *about* her when I'm not there. How'd it go with Eubanks?"

"Not good. Bad, actually." I run a finger through the condensation on the bus's window. "I signed the lease." I hold the phone away from my ear, but I can still hear Iris yelling.

"Are you crazy?"

"Not crazy, just desperate," I say, still holding the phone at arm's length in case of another outburst. "Sometimes they're one and the same."

"And that's what I'll have them put on your tombstone after your mother kills you."

"Don't start planning my funeral. Yet. You home?"

"Just walked through my front door."

"I'm only a couple blocks away from your place. Listen, Iris, there's more, and it's bad."

"How much more and how bad?" I hear her keys land with a clink on her kitchen table.

"We're going to need tequila."

"It's *tequila* bad?"

I sigh. "They're back."

"Who's back?"

The bus stops, and I step out of the way as the door opens to let on more passengers. "Christopher is back in Pointe Hill." After a couple of seconds, I add, "And so is Jason."

The silence on the other end of the line goes on for so long I wonder if the call dropped. "Iris, you still there?"

"Shit," she finally mutters.

"I'll be in front of your building in ten," I say, and use my finger to erase the words I've written in the condensation on the window: *not again*.

CHAPTER FOUR

An empty pan falls to the floor the moment I walk through the back door of the restaurant, and I swear Mom timed it. The metal pan spins on the tile floor, and the vibration echoes in my head as though it's miked.

"You're late!" she yells. Or probably just says, but at six in the morning, my alcohol soaked brain can't tell the difference. Understandable, since I spent the previous night at Iris's place drowning my sorrows in margaritas.

"Sorry," I mutter before reaching for the mug of coffee Anthony is waving under my nose. After taking a gulp of liquid attitude adjustment I say, "I love you."

Anthony places his hands over his heart. "I'm touched."

"I was talking to the coffee." I smile and nudge him when he walks by. Anthony is my brother. Not by blood and not in any legal sense of the word, but when he aged out of foster care and had nowhere else to go, my parents took him in. I was nineteen at the time, a college sophomore consumed with my own problems. For a while, Anthony was just one more example of Agnes and Ray Spalding trying to save the world one person at a time.

But over winter breaks and summers spent working together in the kitchen, Anthony and I forged a bond. One that's become even tighter since I've been back home.

Anthony swats at me, and I duck out of the way, slamming my hip against the long wooden counter in the middle of the restaurant's small kitchen.

"Damn," I mumble, rubbing the sore spot on my side.

"Freedom Isabelle Spalding." The way Mom says my full name, slowly emphasizing each syllable, her Jamaican accent pronouncing the "dom" in Freedom as "dum," is her way of reminding me that even at twenty-four, I'm not too old to be scolded.

"I swear you could hear an ant scratch its head," I say, shaking my head at the woman's superhuman hearing.

Without missing a beat my mom says, "Ants can't reach their heads, and you know how I feel about that kind of language."

I watch her as she moves quickly to the stove to shift the pot of green bananas that are about to boil over. It's sweltering in the kitchen, yet Agnes Spalding looks more like the host of her own cooking show than the owner of Pointe Hill's only Jamaican restaurant. And even with the streak of gray running through the front of her short, curly hair, she looks more like my older sister than my fifty-three-year-old mother. But there are dark circles under her eyes that weren't there before, and I can see the stress of the past year has taken a toll on her.

"No time to fool around this morning. We're already behind schedule." She juts her chin at the mound of mottled yellow-and-black plantains waiting to be peeled.

I prop my sunglasses up on my head.

"Daaamn," Anthony drawls, shaking his head at the

sight of what I can only guess are my swollen, bloodshot eyes.

I raise the hand that isn't holding the coffee mug and offer Anthony a one-finger salute just as Mom looks in our direction.

She frowns and curls her index finger, making a *come here* motion. Anthony grabs a basket of silverware and heads through the swinging doors toward the front of the restaurant. Weighed down by the gallon of margaritas still sloshing around my system, I don't move quickly enough to avoid the steely glare of Agnes Spalding's brown eyes. I'm about to apologize for my language and my lateness when she places a plate of food on the counter and motions for me to sit.

Even hungover, the smell of salted codfish and boiled dumplings causes my stomach to growl. I slide onto the stool and Mom reaches over to smooth my hair, but I duck out of her reach and pull her hand into mine. Her skin is dusted white with flour, and I brush the flour away, gently massaging her hand. Her fingers are as slim as the rest of her and her skin looks smooth, even under the harsh fluorescent kitchen light, but her palms are rough and calloused from years spent in the kitchen. I squeeze her hand and remember what Dad used to say about cooking for people you care about: "The food says I love you, even when you can't."

"I take it things didn't go well yesterday." She hands me a fork and takes the seat across from me. We open at seven, and I feel guilty taking the time to eat, knowing that Mom and Anthony have probably been here since five. But this morning my hunger outweighs my guilt.

"What makes you say that?" I ask, around a mouthful of food.

"Yesterday, you stormed out of here so determined, if you'd gotten him to give you an extension on the old lease, you would have called me right after you left his office."

I pause with the fork midway between the plate and my mouth. Showing up late this morning isn't the only thing I have to feel guilty about. I clear my throat, preparing to explain why I signed a lease committing us to rent we can't afford, when a high-pitch whining interrupts my train of thought. I glance at the ancient freezer, which has been a staple in this kitchen for as long as I can remember. My mom kisses her teeth, and the sharp sound of the air flowing through her teeth lasts longer than the sound coming from the freezer.

"Mom, don't start. It's still got a lot of life in it yet."

She kisses her teeth again. "We need to think about how and when we're going to shut down, Freedom. I've talked to the Makaos and they're willing to buy some of our equipment. Anthony's checked into a couple of places, too. He's been such a godsend, stepping up the way he has. Did you notice he's wearing the hearing aid today? I think he's getting more comfortable with it."

"Mom—"

"He's so self-conscious about it," she continues, her concern for Anthony momentarily trumping thoughts about the restaurant.

"How can you talk about us shutting down like it's no big deal?" The stool scrapes against the tile floor as I push back from the counter. I abandon my half-eaten plate of food and grab my hairnet and apron from the hook on the back of the office door. "Can't you see what's going on?"

Mom doesn't answer. Instead, she takes a stack of paper napkins and begins folding them into neat rectangles.

I gesture to the street in front of the restaurant. "CHI

wants to replace everything that makes the Old Sixth Ward authentic, with a bunch of restaurants and shops that half the people around here can't even afford to patronize. You do know what they'll probably put here if we leave, don't you?" I ask, not waiting for an answer. "An Island Shack. That awful chain of upscale," I use air quotes around the word *upscale*, "Caribbean restaurants from those guys who lost that reality cooking show competition. CHI thinks it can replace Cecelia's with a couple of guys who think that saying, 'hey mon' in a passable Jamaican accent qualifies them to run a Caribbean restaurant. Well, that's bullshit."

Mom's continued silence, even at my use of an expletive, stops me. "Mom?"

She sighs and stops folding the napkins. "I know you think I'm wrong, Free, but it will be better this way. You can move on with your life, and I can move on with mine."

I start shoving utensils into a container to take to the front. "I don't get why you're not more upset about this. Why you're so willing to throw away twenty years of what you and Daddy built together. I glance up my dad's picture on the wall, then at the picture of my paternal grandmother, the restaurant's namesake. "If Daddy were here—"

"But your father is not here." Mom takes a step toward me, absently rubbing her empty ring finger with the thumb of her right hand. "That last stroke," she begins, then swallows hard before continuing. "He's been gone for almost a year now, Free. We *have* to accept that."

The harshness in her voice and the way she says "gone," like Daddy chose to leave us, strikes me like an open hand. Mom sees my reaction and moves toward me, but I back away.

"I didn't mean it like that, Free. I still miss Raymond

every day, but I don't know how we can keep going like this. I don't know if we should."

I take a deep breath and, as always, the aromas of the kitchen play on my emotions. The pepperiness of the jerk seasoning and the bite of the yellow curry ignite my anger, while the sweet smell of sugar buns and plantains salve my foul mood. My voice is measured when I finally speak. "I know it's been difficult without him, Mom. And I know he kind of left us with a mess, but if we just keep working—"

"Then what? We make it through the first month and maybe the next." Her voice is strained as she looks around the kitchen then back at me. "Then what?"

"And then we make it through the next, and then the next, and then . . ." But the truth is I don't know what happens after that. I'm struggling to come up with an answer when the swinging doors that lead from the front of the restaurant to the kitchen open. Mom and I retreat, she to the oven to check on the batch of sugar buns she's baking, me to the pile of plantains.

"I know it's a little early, but Mr. and Mrs. Dawson are already waiting outside. Can I open up now?" Anthony asks.

"Sure, dear. We don't want to keep anyone waiting."

Anthony pauses, but says nothing before heading back to the front. He's used to hearing us argue, but it always makes him uncomfortable.

When he's gone, my mother says, "Well, it doesn't matter now. The window to renew the lease is closed, so whether you agree with me or not, we move forward. There's nothing more to say."

Tiny beads of sweat have formed across her top lip, and a light sheen covers her face. Her words may have sounded confident, but the expression on her face is anything but.

And it's not just the heat of the kitchen; Mom is tired. That realization presses the pause button on my anger. I can't tell her right now. Not about signing the lease and definitely not about Christopher. What I want to tell her is that I love her, and I'm sorry we're not closer.

I turn my attention to the stove instead, watching the oil pop in the frying pan. The plantains are dark and crispy around the edges, but the centers of the oval-shaped discs are uncooked. I let the oil get too hot. Dad didn't make mistakes like that. His fried plantains were perfect every time. I turn down the flame.

"You're burning them," Mom says, over her shoulder, reminding me that I'm not the only one who knows I'll never be able to fill my father's shoes.

CHAPTER FIVE

The walking basslines of ska waft from the restaurant's speakers and help set the pace as we work through the morning rush. My headache from earlier, the fight I had with Mom, and thoughts of Christopher, all fade as I give in to the rhythm of prep work.

I've lost track of time when Cassie, the daughter of one of my mom's friends, pops her head in the kitchen to tell me Simone has arrived. Cassie started working for us the summer before her senior year in high school. Now she's a sophomore at Pointe Hill College, and since I've been back, she's been indispensable in helping me get back up to speed at the restaurant.

I glance up at the clock. "Shoot," I say, "she's early."

"Did you get a chance to try out the braised jerked wings recipe I told you about?" Cassie asks as I pull my hairnet off and yank my apron over my head.

"Sorry, Cass, I've been swamped. I promise, if we get this gig, it'll be the first item we add to the menu."

"Who is *that*?" Anthony asks, flicking his thumb toward

the front of the restaurant, when I almost run into him on my way out of the kitchen.

"She's here for a tasting. Why?"

He shrugs. "She's hot," he says.

I swat him with a dish towel as I head through the doors.

Simone is standing close to the entrance, her arm crooked around the handle of a large leather handbag. She fidgets with the colorful silk scarf around her neck as her eyes scan the restaurant. I follow her gaze, seeing the faded wallpaper and mismatched chairs, tables smooth and shiny from two decades of diners' hands. Behind the counter, the green and yellow of the Jamaican flag, bleached in a striped pattern that matches the sunlight coming through the blinds on the front door. Even the Bob Marley poster, a contractual obligation for every Jamaican restaurant, has paled over time.

"Simone," I say, extending a hand as I approach her. "So glad you could make it."

"Sure thing," she says, shaking my hand and scanning me much the way she did the restaurant.

The door to the small office closes as I enter the kitchen, and I know Mom's avoiding me. I lead Simone to the two trays of appetizers I have displayed on the counter. The savory tray has mini beef patties, festival, saltfish fritters, and jerk chicken wings. The sweet tray features miniature versions of rock cakes with grated coconuts, cupcake-sized bun and cheese sandwiches, and plantain tarts.

I pull out a stool. "Please, have a seat. I can't wait to have you try these. They're some of our most popular dishes."

As Simone bends to inspect the trays, her long, dark hair fans out over her shoulder. I recognize the designer label on the purse she's got tucked under her arm because Iris has one just like it.

"They certainly look interesting. May I?" she asks, pointing to one of the patties.

"Of course."

Simone pinches the edge of the patty's crust and delicately places it into her mouth. She chews the quarter inch piece of crust as though she's just shoved an entire steak into her mouth.

"How many calories are in one of these?"

"Calories? I don't know offhand, I could review the recipe—"

"Our clientele is becoming more health conscious. I mean, who can blame them, right? I wish I could afford not to care about calories." I swear her eyes linger on my hips when she says this.

"Well, I can certainly get those numbers for you." I place a plantain tart on a napkin and hand it to her.

Simone waves it away. "Plantain tart, right? I've had those before. Do you have anything ... different?"

"Different how?"

"I was in Atlanta not too long ago and stopped by that new place, Montego's. Their menu is amazing. They had lamb patties and jerk pork pot-stickers. Really authentic stuff, you know?"

"I think I'd know a thing or two about authentic Jamaican food. I may not have been born there, but I've been eating the food since I was in a high chair." I smile and pop a plantain tart in my mouth to stop myself from saying anything I'd regret.

"Yes, of course," Simone says with a nervous laugh. "It's just that the neighborhood landscape is changing, and I think anyone who wants to keep up with it should adapt."

Cecelia's menu is as authentic as it gets. When he was alive, my father made daily trips outside of Pointe Hill to the international farmers' market, even though there was a market much closer. That market had items like scotch bonnet peppers, sorrel, coconuts, things he couldn't get anywhere else. Now my mom and I make the trips.

"Why don't you try one of the wings?" I move the tray closer to her.

She eyes the tray, but shakes her head. "I'm in a bit of a hurry. Maybe you can pack this up and I'll take it with me? I'm sure someone back at the office will appreciate it."

"Sure," I stutter, taken aback that she's come all the way here and has sampled only one item.

She must notice the change in my expression because she adds, "It all looks good, but I had lunch with a client before I got here, and I'm one of those people watching my waistline."

I remember that Iris said this meeting was just a formality and try to smile as a few minutes later, and less than fifteen minutes after she arrived, Simone exits the restaurant with a small takeout bag.

By the time Simone leaves, the lunch crowd is gone and we're just about to close up for the day. I watch as Mom walks Sam to the door. She throws her head back and laughs at something he says.

"Mom," I call to her, and when she looks up with a scowl on her face, I realize I sounded harsher than I'd intended to. Sam glances my way and waves, says something to Mom, then leaves.

"That was very rude, Freedom. I raised you better than

that," Mom says when she comes to stand next to me at the counter.

I push through the swinging doors and she follows me into the kitchen.

"Why haven't you put your ring back on?"

"What?" she asks, spinning to face me even as her right hand floats up to her ring finger.

I point to her hand. "Your wedding ring. You took it off on Monday."

"I take it off whenever I have a lot of baking to do."

"Well, it's Saturday and you still haven't put it back on."

My mother is silent.

"Is that why you didn't want to sign the lease?"

Mom looks up at me, a warning in her eyes. "Is what why?"

"Sam. Are you and Sam . . ." I trail off, unwilling to finish the sentence.

"Are Sam and I *what*, Freedom? You bold enough to start this conversation with your mother, be bold enough to finish it. Are we what?"

I pick up a rag and start wiping at a grease stain so hard the pots rattle.

"Are we what?" Mom repeats, tugging my elbow until I'm facing her.

My mother is shorter than I am, but whenever she looks at me the way she's looking at me now, I feel like the little one.

My voice hitches, but I answer anyway. "Is he the reason you stopped caring about the restaurant? Why you were so ready to give up?"

"Give up? You have no idea how hard I've worked to keep this place going. I'm the reason your father could hone those recipes he was so loved for." She taps her chest. "I was the one making sure the bills got paid, pleading with merchants for extensions. All so your father could fulfill his dream."

I open then close my mouth, grasping for the right words. "So you don't care anymore because this was his dream and not yours?"

"Stop telling me I don't care!" Mom yells. She points up to my grandmother's picture on the wall. "Your grandmother spent every single day of her adult life behind four walls cooking for customers, taking care of your father and his brother, denying her own dreams so they could pursue theirs. When she sent your father here to the States, this restaurant was her dream for him. A dream I worked hard to help him fulfill. And this restaurant was his dream for you." She lowers her voice, decompressing as if the air has been let out of her. "Before you left, anyway."

I feel equal parts guilt for leaving them and anger for their expectation that I wouldn't, and that lifelong internal tug of war brings tears to my eyes.

"After you left, I did the best I could," Mom says. "I don't think you know how much we sacrificed for you. How much *I* sacrificed."

"Maybe that's the problem. Dad never made me feel like anything he did for me was a sacrifice, and you make me feel like everything you do is." I toss the dishrag down on the counter and scrub my hands over my face. "I don't want to have this fight with you again, Mom. Not today."

She sighs and walks over, taking my hands in hers, studying them for a long while before saying, "Your dad wanted this life for you, but I never did. Getting up early every morning, working in a hot kitchen all day . . ." She runs her fingers along the ridge of a scar on the palm of my left hand. "Remember how you got this?" Her soft brown eyes, mirror images of my own, are wet when she looks up at me. "You cut yourself when you were eleven or twelve. You were so determined to help your dad prep for a party he was catering," she presses gently on the scar, "and you just sliced right through it with his knife."

I remember the day clearly. My being in the kitchen that day wasn't just about helping Daddy. It was an apology. One I'm not even sure I realized I was making at the time.

Mom lifts my other hand and turns it over so my palm faces down. She runs her fingers along the dark spots that dot my skin. "And you always burn yourself with the oil."

Standing this close to her I see the lines that have just recently begun to form at the corners of her mouth, the fine crows' feet at the corners of her eyes.

"The spots will fade, Mom, they always do." I place a hand on her cheek, using my thumb to smooth over the frown lines on her face.

After a beat, she says, "You seem anxious today. Was it your meeting yesterday?"

I nod, staring down at her hand still clasping mine. "Let me try one last time before you give up on this place. I need to do this. I need you to let me try."

Mom hesitates, and in that moment, a sliver of hope floats in the air between us. She pats my hand. "I've already made my decision, Free."

I pull my hands away and pick up the dishcloth. "And so have I. I signed the lease."

MOM HAS BEEN SILENTLY FUMING SINCE I TOLD HER about the lease, vigorously scrubbing the kitchen counter instead of talking to me. This is Mom in denial mode. After

Dad's stroke, when it was clear to everyone else he wouldn't have the strength to keep working at the restaurant, she spent hours mopping floors and shining windows so things would be "perfect for him when he was ready to come back."

"Mom," I plead, trailing behind her as she cleans. "We can't give up yet. Anthony's going to get word about the catering contract with Pointe Hill State's mentoring program any day now. And Iris says we're a lock for the Solstice job." I omit the part about Simone turning her nose up at our menu.

Mom stops short and turns. "You went behind my back and signed the lease. You had no right to do that."

"We are equal owners now that Dad is gone. I had every right to sign that lease."

She purses her lips, and looks as though she's about to say something, but returns to her scrubbing without saying a word. When she hears what I'm about to tell her, we're going to be able to eat off the floor. "There's something else you should know, Mom."

She stops scrubbing, but doesn't look up.

"I tried to get the rent lowered, but I don't think there was anything I could have said that would have persuaded Eubanks to give us an extension. We know him."

"I don't know anyone named—"

"It's Christopher." I clear my throat before continuing, but my voice still sounds croaky when I say, "Christopher Bellamy."

She finally stops scrubbing and looks at me, her face paling. "Christopher?"

"Mom, you okay?"

"Christopher Bellamy? Are you sure?"

"He's taken his father's last name now, but it's him."

"What did he say?"

I fill Mom in on the details of Christopher's return, leaving out the round of mutual father bashing.

Mom is quiet for so long, I touch her hand.

"How was it, seeing him again?" she asks.

If there's an upside to mentioning Christopher, it's that it seems to put a pin in the conversation about the lease. I take the dishrag to the sink and start rinsing it. "It was fine. I'm fine," I say. "I'm not some lovesick teenager anymore."

"Still, it was cruel what he did to you. You didn't talk to me about it much, but I knew he was your first love. And then to do that . . . after you'd spent all that money on that prom dress. I don't know why he thought he could just show up here the next morning and—"

The faucet is still running when I turn to face her. "What do you mean 'just show up here'?"

"Well not here, the house—"

"What do you mean *just show up here*?"

Mom's voice drops to a whisper. "I've always wondered if you knew. If Christopher had found a way to get to you after—"

"After what?" My headache is back, twisting its tendrils up the back of my neck and branching out across my forehead.

"Raymond said—"

"Daddy? What does he have to do with this?"

"You have to understand why we did it."

"Did what, Mom? What did you do?"

Mom straightens and clears her throat. Behind me, the water gurgles from the faucet.

"The morning after your prom, Christopher came to the house looking for you. Your dad told him you never wanted to see him again."

CHAPTER SIX

"Christopher came to the house? Where was I? Why didn't you get me?"

"His brother had only brought you home a few hours earlier. You were crying and you'd obviously been drinking. We got you upstairs and you'd finally just fallen asleep."

"You should have gotten me. And Daddy knew?"

"Your father was the one who answered the door."

I rest my head on the counter. Christopher had come for me. Maybe he'd come to apologize. Maybe he'd come to explain why he'd shown up at the prom with Jessica Riley only weeks after telling me he loved me. "What did he say?" I ask, my head still bowed.

"Your father only told me about it after Christopher had already left. He said Christopher was upset. Your father thought maybe he'd been drinking, too. Said he'd been rambling on about his mother and his brother, about a mistake."

Her fingers graze my hand and I pull away from her. "So Dad just let him leave and neither of you ever said a word to me about it."

"Believe it or not, we were thinking about you, Free. Do you remember what you were like the first time Christopher walked out of your life? You barely ate. You didn't sleep. Your grades fell so badly we were scared you'd have to repeat your senior year. We'd finally gotten you back, then he shows up and hurts you again. You were in no position to make any rational decisions that morning."

"So you made them for me."

Mom stands a little straighter. "Yes. And I'd do it again if I thought it would protect you."

My head and heart are pounding. I close my eyes and imagine what the past several years of my life would have been like had I seen Christopher that morning. "Oh God, Mom, maybe he and I would have . . ." I flounder for the right words. "Maybe I would have avoided some of the mistakes I made after I left Pointe Hill."

"What mistakes? What are you talking about?" Mom asks, her hands twisting the strings of her apron. When I don't answer, her tone changes. "I suppose I'm to blame for those mistakes too." She unties the apron and walks to the office. When she returns, she's holding her purse and car keys.

"You're leaving?" I follow her through the kitchen door to the front of the restaurant. "So that's it? That's all you have to say about this?"

Mom stops and swivels to face me. "You're not the only one sick of fighting. But I'll tell you this; I was *not* going to let that boy hurt you again. And you know what? It's time you were honest with yourself."

"What does *that* mean?"

"It means that if Christopher had really wanted to see you again, had *really* wanted to be with you, he would have found a way not an excuse."

Her words knock the momentum out of my anger, throwing me off balance, and I lean against the side of one of the booths.

Mom pulls a chain from around her neck. Her wedding band dangles from it. "I put the ring on a chain because it's easier for me to keep track of it this way."

Still reeling from what she's just said about Christopher, I swallow the lump in my throat and mumble a feeble, "Okay."

"But Freedom, if and when I decide it's time to stop wearing my wedding ring, it will be my decision and mine alone. And it will have nothing to do with how much I loved your father."

She heads through the front door and I start to follow her but my phone rings. I grab it without checking the caller ID. "Yes?"

"Whoa, what's gotten into you?" Iris asks.

"You wouldn't believe me if I told you."

"Christopher and Jason have a third, even more assholey brother they didn't tell us about?"

Despite the heavy conversation I've just had with Mom, I chuckle. "No, but it has to do with them. I'll tell you later. What's up?"

"I think I've got a plan to help you hang on to the restaurant."

"At this point, I'm willing to try just about anything. Let's hear it," I say, taking a seat at a booth in front of the large window that faces the street. It's after four, and people are beginning to trickle out of office buildings into the swamp-like humidity. The men loosen their ties and the women remove the sweaters they donned to survive the day in the arctic environment of their air-conditioned offices.

"A bunch of us at Solstice were invited to an event next Tuesday night."

"My life is circling down the drain and you want me to go to a party? Iris, I'm still hungover from last night. I can't bounce back from these things the way you do. Hard pass for me."

"Really? Even if the fabulous Bellamy boys will be there, along with all the free press you can shake a finger at?"

I sit up straighter. "I'm listening."

"It's not an account I'm managing so I didn't know about the invite until today, but Solstice is handling one of CHI's launch events. The event is being held at The Depot —you know, that old train station they just renovated—and I can get you in. CHI representatives will be talking about phase two of their development project and taking questions from attendees."

"And I could use the opportunity to ask about the negative impact their projects have been having on the community."

"Exactly. If you handle it right, Cecelia's will get some positive press and you might even knock those arrogant Bellamy boys down a notch or two."

"And if I don't handle it right?"

"What do you have to lose?"

I look outside at the sidewalk full of people heading home after productive workdays, and my stomach flutters. I have no job to go back to, no one waiting for me when I get home. Cecelia's is all I have left, and if I lose that, I'll have nothing. "More than you know, Iris. More than you know."

CHAPTER SEVEN

"Remind me why I let you convince me to come to this thing," I say, groaning and leaning my head against the sleek leather of Iris's passenger seat as she swings her car into a parking spot at The Depot.

When she cuts the engine but doesn't move to get out of the car, drumming her fingers against the steering wheel instead, I look at her. The bangs of her pixie cut hide her eyes, so all I see are the tips of her dark eyelashes fluttering against her high cheekbones, and a long, silver earring shimmering against her brown skin. "I thought I was the one who didn't want to go inside."

She stills her hands and stares at her fingernails. This week's manicure color is a deep, dark purple that in the dimly lit car looks almost black. "You know if I had the money, I'd give it to you, right?"

As kids, if I'd been the poster child for Goodwill, Iris had been Gucci's. Her father, Nicholas Hauss, a respected German photographer, and my aunt Petra—his manager—raised her in New York City on a steady diet of debutante balls and designer labels.

That all changed when Uncle Nick decided he'd had enough. He moved back to Germany, sold most of his possessions, and kissed that lifestyle goodbye. The marriage didn't withstand the change, and Iris was given three options: move to Jamaica with her mom, live in Germany with her dad, or come to Georgia to live with us. Iris chose Georgia, although she never quite got the high life out of her system. My Mom always said Iris had champagne taste and Coca-Cola money. After I moved away from Pointe Hill, Iris and I didn't spend much time together, only reconnecting after I returned. But if her car and weekly mani and pedi are any indication, not much has changed as far as her tastes.

"Even if you could lend me the money, I wouldn't let you. You've wanted to launch your event-planning business for years. You need money as much as I do."

Iris runs her palms along the steering wheel. "I know, it's just . . . I wish I could do more."

"You've done more than anyone else has. You're the reason Cecelia's was even considered for the Solstice gig. Although I think I might have blown it with Simone."

"Don't worry about Simone. She might be in charge," Iris makes air quotes with her fingers when she says *in charge*, "but I still have a lot of pull with Garrett."

"Thanks." I grab her hand and squeeze it.

She squeezes back. "We'll figure it out. And it starts with us getting out of this car."

Iris jumps out, and her heels click on the asphalt as she walks around to the passenger side and pulls my door open. "And, to answer your question, you came here tonight because you know I'm always right about these things."

Iris offers her hand and I take it, stepping out of the car and teetering on a pair of her heels she insisted I wear. I adjust the neckline of my dress, also from her closet. The dress is fitted, with the top exposing the kind of cleavage I don't ever have to worry about in jeans and a T-shirt.

Iris smacks my hands away, undoing the button I just did. "You're not interviewing for a position at a nunnery."

"I'm not interviewing for a position as a wet nurse, either."

"Good, because you definitely wouldn't get the job all buttoned up like that." Satisfied with my shirt to cleavage ratio, Iris steps back, looks me over from head to toe, and nods approvingly at her handiwork.

"Okay," I say, exhaling a long, slow breath.

"Try not to look so nervous."

"Of course I'm nervous, it's only my future at stake here."

"You're going to be great. The press is going to eat it up when you talk about Cecelia's and what places like it mean to this community. No company wants bad press. CHI might even revisit the new lease terms."

"I hope you're right."

"I know I'm right. And when Christopher gets one look at you in that dress—"

"I don't care what Christopher thinks about me *or* this dress."

"Yeah, keep telling yourself that," Iris says, grinning. "The last time he saw you, you had flour on your ass and pit stains on your shirt." When I balk, Iris says, "Your words, not mine. It's time to let him see what he's missed out on all these years."

"My feet are already killing me. Can we go inside now?" I say, swallowing the nerves already eating at my gut.

Inside The Depot, the low buzz of after-work business chatter mingles with the sound of soft jazz. Exposed beams and mortar-smeared brick walls make the space seem larger than it looks from the outside.

Iris spots her colleagues and introduces me. Simone greets me with a subdued smile, and I make a mental note to grill Iris later about anything Simone says tonight about the gig. When Iris and her coworkers start talking shop, I excuse myself and begin examining the pictures hanging on the walls.

The photos are mostly of old train stations and railroad cars, but several are of travelers from a bygone era. One of the photos is of a young girl standing under a sign that reads "Coloreds Only." She's staring at the camera, and her sweet innocence is in stark contrast to the ugly reality that hangs above her head. The image of the girl in her simple cotton dress is even more striking set against the backdrop of this well-heeled crowd.

"Champagne?" a server asks, seeming to materialize out of nowhere. He hands me a glass and I take a long swallow, the bubbles tickling my nose as they fizz and burst. I search for Iris in the growing crowd, and that's when I see him.

Christopher is across the room, one hand propped against a wooden column, the other wrapped around a glass of amber liquid. He's sporting a five o' clock shadow and a dark, slim-cut suit. One, that by the looks of it, has been tailor-made for him. His head is bent, and he's looking down at a beautiful brunette who gazes up at him adoringly.

When the woman rises on her toes and whispers something in his ear, a pang of an emotion I don't dare define slices through me like a hot knife through butter. Christopher scans the room as she speaks, and our eyes meet before I can look away. I watch as his expression slides from blank, to puzzled, to annoyed, before settling on amused.

As he watches me, he leans in and whispers something

into the woman's ear that makes her toss her head back and laugh. I fight the urge to walk over and throw the contents of my glass in his smug face. Instead, I raise my glass, nod in his direction, and take a sip. Christopher looks right at me as he traces the tip of his finger along the curve of the woman's neck before twirling a lock of her hair around his finger. I lower my glass and roll my eyes so hard I almost pull a muscle. I've got to find Iris.

A few minutes after I make my way back to Iris, Christopher's deep voice booms from speakers located on a stage at the front of the room. "Ladies and gentlemen, my brother Jason and I would like to thank you for coming out tonight. At CHI, community has always come first, and tonight with the opening of this incubator space, we reconfirm our commitment to the continued growth and revitalization of Pointe Hill."

It takes a second for me to realize that the man joining Christopher on stage is Jason. He's walking with a slight limp, and Jason 2.0 looks less like the muscle-bound jock he was in high school and more like a distance runner. The sight of the brothers together causes my breath to hitch.

"Well, damn," Iris whispers. "Those are two fine sons of a—"

"Shh!" A woman standing in front of us says, turning toward us and placing her forefinger against her lips.

Iris raises a brow, and I stifle a laugh as Christopher continues. "CHI's continued investment in this community will add much needed dollars to its economy, improve its schools, and significantly enhance the services Pointe Hill will be able to provide its residents."

Christopher talks for several minutes, repeating the refrain about commitment to community so many times, I wonder if his record has skipped. Fifteen minutes and three additional commitments to community's later he opens the floor to questions.

A handful of reporters, including the brunette from earlier, lob softball questions at the brothers, who take turns answering. Iris elbows me when there's a lull between questions and my hand instinctively shoots up even as I elbow her back.

At first I don't think Christopher is going to acknowledge me, but he soon walks to the edge of the stage and nods in my direction. The look he gives me could give the devil chills.

"Ms. Spalding," he says, nodding.

I take a deep breath then begin. "Before his death, my father, Raymond Spalding, and my mother, Agnes, ran Cecelia's, the Jamaican restaurant in the Old Sixth Ward. Like a lot of small businesses in this community, my parents built their restaurant from the ground up and have been fixtures here for almost twenty years. But your recent actions have already forced several businesses like theirs to relocate and others to close their doors all together. These are businesses that were instrumental in building Pointe Hill . . ."

Christopher steps down from the stage and approaches me, his laser-like gaze focused on me. His intense expression makes me momentarily lose track, but I quickly regain my train of thought. "These original businesses were staples in the community, employing individuals and providing jobs when larger establishments stayed away."

Christopher draws nearer. "Do you have a question, Ms. Spalding?"

I look around at the faces staring at me, then over at the picture of the little girl on the wall. "There are people in the community, particularly those who remember a time when there were only a few places where they were welcomed, who don't want to see businesses like ours leave. CHI, and developers like yours, are pricing these residents and businesses right out of Pointe Hill."

A few *yeses* rise from the audience, emboldening me to continue. "You can't put paint and mortar on what you're doing and call it progress if it ignores large portions of the community. You asked for a question, well here it is: does making it almost impossible for these businesses to stay here *really* benefit the community or does it just benefit your bottom line?"

There's a pause as all eyes and cameras, turn to Christopher. A chorus of murmurs and head nods lets me know my comments have struck a chord.

Christopher takes a few more steps in my direction. "The businesses in that area have been given the option to remain if—"

"At rents you know most of us can't afford. Maybe if you'd give us more time to adjust to the changes and extend the previous lease terms, we could work with you toward an outcome that genuinely benefits the community," I say.

Christopher is standing so close now, I can see the patch of gray hair over his left ear, the one he's had since high school. The crowd is quiet, my own breathing the only sound I hear.

"The marketplace is becoming extremely competitive and unfortunately, businesses that can't manage to keep up will have a difficult time surviving."

The arrogance in his tone infuriates me. "You—"

"Free," Jason's voice projects through the speakers, and I glance at him. He's calm, his features relaxed. He nods and after a few beats, I nod, too, acknowledging a time when we weren't on opposing sides. He continues. "We're dedicated to working with Pointe Hill's citizens as we develop this project. I'm sure my brother can make time to meet with you to discuss our plans in greater detail."

Christopher doesn't budge, and neither do I.

"Ladies and gentlemen," Jason says. "We'll be wrapping things up soon, but please take a minute to introduce yourself to the CHI staff and learn more about our initiatives. Thank you for coming out this evening."

The crowd applauds, and it's only when a handful of reporters surround me, that Christopher walks away. I spend the next several minutes answering questions.

After the reporters leave, a hand on my arm and a soft-spoken "Ms. Spalding," get my attention. A smartly dressed woman a little older than my mother extends a petite hand toward me.

"I'm Sandra Kane, chair of the Pointe Hill Chamber of Commerce. Your father was a regular at our meetings. He bragged about his college graduate daughter all the time."

The mention of my father's name brings a familiar lump to my throat. "Thank you, Mrs. Kane."

"Please, call me Sandra. Free, I'd like to invite you to speak at our next chamber meeting. A group of us have been organizing a special committee to address our concerns about the uptick in development in Pointe Hill."

She rests a hand on my shoulder and ushers me to a quiet area off to the side of the room. "We're looking for someone to head the committee. With your education and the concern you've shown here tonight, I think you'd be perfect in the role."

"I'd love to come to the meeting."

Sandra and I exchange contact information and as I watch her walk away, I feel something I haven't felt in a long time—optimism.

I'm waiting for Iris to wrap things up with her colleagues when I spot a lone glass of champagne sitting on a tray. I make a beeline for the table and grab the glass before a server can whisk it away. I can almost taste the bubbly on my tongue when a large, warm hand wraps around my arm, halting the glass midway to my lips.

"That was quite a performance." Christopher breathes the words into my ear.

Despite the venom in his voice, his lips are upturned in what a casual observer would mistake as a smile. When he steps back to appraise me, his eyes linger on the neckline of my dress. I send a telepathic thank you to Iris.

"I'm glad you enjoyed it." I jerk my elbow from his grip and sip my champagne. "The performance, I mean."

"*Enjoyed* isn't the word that comes to mind." His eyes meet mine. "The performance, I mean."

"What word would you use? Relished? Appreciated? Delighted in?"

Christopher chuckles before stepping closer. "You don't want to do this, Freedom. Not with me, not now."

"True, vocabulary was never your strong suit."

He laughs again, but the laugh doesn't reach his eyes.

Movement behind him catches my attention, and I see the brunette reporter he was being chummy with earlier shooting daggers at me with her eyes.

I raise my chin in her direction. "I think your groupie is looking for you."

Christopher doesn't even turn to look. "Which one?"

"Touché. You *have* always had a problem settling for just one, haven't you?"

He moves even closer, his voice a low hiss. "What the hell do you think you're playing at?" A server walks up to take my glass just as I'm about to answer Christopher.

Before I can tell the server I'm not done with my drink, Christopher takes it, places it on the tray, then grabs my elbow.

"What do you think you're doing?" I ask.

"Taking you somewhere we can talk. In private."

———————

CHAPTER EIGHT

C hristopher tugs me into a small office away from the main meeting area and slams the door behind him. The room smells like paint and freshly lain carpet, a single desk and chair are against the wall across from the door. I toss my clutch onto the desk and look around.

"Disappointed there's nothing in here you can throw at me?" Christopher asks.

"Don't underestimate me. That desk probably isn't as heavy as it looks." I rest my hands on my hips. "What do you want?"

"That was a nice show, Free. Very heartfelt. But there are no cameras in here, no press. You can be honest now. Why are you really here?"

"Were you listening to a word I said? I refuse to let you and CHI take everything—"

"No, why are you back in Pointe Hill? You hated this place when we were in high school. Hated everything about it, including the restaurant."

"I didn't hate the restaurant."

Christopher sneers. "Rewriting history won't change what actually happened. You *hated* that restaurant."

His words are unsettling, even if they're only half true. "I hated having to work there every day after school. I hated always smelling like the inside of a kitchen. But I *never* hated the restaurant, I just wanted . . ." I trail off, trying to ignore the feeling that rises in the pit of my stomach every time I think about that period in my life.

Christopher leans against the desk and crosses his legs at the ankles. "You haven't answered my question."

"I came back after my dad had the second stroke. For a while it looked like maybe he'd get better, but he never did. I stayed because my mother needed me."

Christopher shakes his head then stands. "Here's the truth: you can't afford to keep the restaurant going. I know it, your mom seems to know it, and I think you know it, too."

"If you think I can't turn this around, you're in for a surprise."

"Come on, Free, Cecelia's isn't sustainable. Hasn't been in a long time. Your customers aren't exactly big spenders."

"It has always been about money with you, hasn't it? Money isn't everything, Christopher."

He snorts. "There are only two kinds of people who say that—those who've always had enough and those who never will."

My family has always struggled financially and Christopher knows that. I shake my head. "How did I buy the nice guy act for so long? You don't care about anyone but yourself."

His face contorts into a grimace and he jerks a finger in my direction. "You have no *idea* who I care about."

"So, which Christopher came back for me that morning? Was it the caring one?" I ask, throwing up air quotes around the word *caring*. "Or was it the one standing here now? Because if it was this one, I'm glad I wasn't there to see him."

I can tell the moment my words register. His head jerks up, his Adam's apple bobs when he swallows. The vulnerability in his expression causes me to soften my voice when I say, "I didn't realize you'd come to see me that morning. My mother just—"

"Is that what this is all about? Prom? You showing up here tonight, trying to humiliate me at my own event, is about me taking Jessica to the prom instead of you?"

"You arrogant son of a bitch," I sputter. "You think I'd put my family's restaurant on the line because you decided to play dress up with some other girl? Flaking out on me at prom was the least of the promises you broke, and you know it."

Christopher curls his lip. "It's been seven years, Free. I can't believe you're still pining over whatever it was you thought we were."

"I don't miss what we were. I miss what I wanted us to be."

He flinches, his brows pulling inward as he stares at me for several seconds, his expression making him look lost, confused. But then he shakes his head and stands. "Let the lease lapse, Free. I'll pretend you never signed it." He rolls his shoulders and huffs. "And if you agree to be out within the next thirty days, CHI will purchase some of your equipment."

"How magnanimous of you."

Christopher sighs. "I thought you'd be glad to let the place go. Glad to leave Pointe Hill once and for all."

"Things are different now. This is something I have to do."

"And this is something I have to do. Believe me, I wouldn't be back in this place if it wasn't."

"*Believe* and *me* aren't words I'd use in the same sentence if I were you. Not with your track record."

Christopher shakes his head and is about to say something, but seems to switch gears. "What about your plans?"

"What plans?"

"Working your way up through an ad agency. International clients, big contracts, traveling?" He moves closer. Close enough that I can smell the warm caramel of scotch on his breath. So close I have to raise my head to meet his eyes.

He runs his tongue across his bottom lip. "I need this, Free."

The thing with his tongue is a tell. He's nervous. It's something he's done since he first sat across from me in the library in the tenth grade.

"I have contacts. I can get you in at an agency. You'd be making a hell of a lot more money than you do now." He lays his hand on my shoulder. "I remember how badly you wanted that career, Free. Look, let's leave the past in the past, isn't that what you said? We can help each other now." He squeezes my shoulder and stares into my eyes, and I have to work overtime to focus on what he's saying instead of the warmth of his hand against my skin.

Maybe it's because he's standing so close, maybe it's the champagne I've had, but when he runs his tongue over his lips again, I feel the tug. The pull. It's what brought me back to him after the first time he'd cut me out of his life. It's how we ended up sleeping together the one and only time we ever did. And it's what has me breathing in his scent now like it's the air I need to survive.

I lay my hand on his chest and let it sit there, feeling it rise and fall through his shirt.

"Free . . ." His voice is a low hum. The vibration enters through my fingertips and runs through my body, playing it like an instrument. For a few seconds, I close my eyes and succumb to the sensation, allowing my breathing to match his.

This is how he got me before. And this is how he thinks he'll get me again. But there's too much at stake now to allow Christopher to play me like an instrument. Slowly, the caramel smell dissipates, the rubber smell of new carpet and the ammonia of the paint replacing it.

"What you said before about money," I begin, looking up at him, "is wrong. There's another type of person who understands money isn't everything—someone like me. I've seen you get all the money you could ever want, but I know you still have nothing."

I pull my hand off his chest, then reach around him and grab my clutch from the desk. "You have the signed lease, and I'm not changing my mind. Not this week, not next, not ever. If the reception I got this evening is any indication, I have a number of supporters and more than a few positive articles coming out in the press. Extend the previous rental terms, Christopher. Give me and the other businesses time to catch up to the changes happening around us. It would be good press for CHI if you did."

Christopher exhales and adjusts his cufflinks while I wait for his response. Then he walks toward the door, pausing long enough to hand me a business card he's just taken from his jacket. "Take this. You'll need it when you come to your senses," he says before jerking the door open and leaving without saying another word.

I step out of the office and yell after him, "If you adjust

the lease terms, people will think you care about something other than yourself!"

Without even turning, he says, "Unfortunately for you, I don't give a damn what people think about me."

CHAPTER NINE

"I don't know what you guys did last night but it worked." Anthony says, greeting me at the back door with a cup of coffee. When I furrow my brow he tilts his head toward the front of the restaurant. "Go take a look."

I pass Cassie, who's stacking silverware into containers to stock the tables, and peek through the swinging doors. Besides our regular breakfast crowd, I see quite a few new faces and several people waiting to be seated.

"I can't believe how busy we are," Cassie says. "We should really get some of those newer items on the menu, Free. I feel like we're missing out on a great opportunity here. I've been looking into—"

"I figured I'd picked up a few supporters last night, but I didn't expect anything this quickly." I let the door swing shut. "I'm sorry, Cass. What were you saying?"

"Doesn't matter. Whatever you said last night worked, old menu or not." Anthony says.

Cassie glances at Anthony and lets out a puff of air, blowing strands of her wheat-colored hair out of her eyes.

Her ever-present headphones hang from her neck, the music a tinny sound in the background.

Anthony pulls his phone out of his apron pocket and taps it a couple of times. "I have to head back out front, but I think you probably have this blog post to thank."

Anthony hands me his phone. It's open to the home page of the *Pointe Hill Post*, the town's most popular website for news and gossip. Below the masthead is a picture of me at last night's event. I read the accompanying headline aloud. "Local Owner Promises Fight."

I look at Mom, who's just stepped out of the pantry. She's shaking her head. "Don't dash 'way your stick before you finish crossing the river, Free," she says as she places two large bags of flour on the prep counter.

Mom has spent most of her adult life here in the States, but she's quick with a Jamaican proverb when it suits her. This is her way of telling me not to celebrate prematurely. Then she adds, "But we've got new customers out there now, so let's make sure they get what they came here for." She says this gruffly, but there's a hint of a smile on her face. I know we're going to have to talk about Christopher and the lease soon, but for now, the crowd out front is a welcome distraction.

I skim the article. It calls Cecelia's one of Pointe Hill's hidden gems, and as I grab my apron and start prepping for the lunch rush, I chuckle because Daddy would have balked at Cecelia's being called "hidden." I tuck the phone in my pocket and head back to the kitchen, tapping my hand against my thigh to the beat of the song playing through the speakers.

We're busy all morning and into the late afternoon. My fingers are sore from chopping and prepping pounds of veggies and potatoes, and I've burned myself on the stove, again. But the exhaustion I feel is tempered by the satisfaction I get from creating something people enjoy. Daddy used to talk about that feeling all the time, but I didn't fully understand it until recently.

By the time two-thirty rolls around, there are only two people left in the restaurant, so I head to the register to begin closing out, passing Anthony behind the counter. He's deep in conversation with a girl with a mane of dark, curly hair. She's seated at the counter, her foot slowly rotating the stool from side to side. He's leaning in, his elbows resting on the counter, chin cupped in his hands. I chuckle and waggle my eyebrows, eliciting a "scram" head-tilt from Anthony.

I've just shoved a couple of tamarind balls into my mouth and I'm in full squirrel-storing-acorns mode, when a guy who looks about my age walks up to the counter.

"That was amazing," he says, handing me a twenty. "I've never had ackee and saltfish before." He stretches out the *double-e* in *ackee* so it sounds like he's saying *a key*.

I chuckle. "Pretend it's spelled with an *ie* instead of a *double-e*."

He says it again, perfectly this time, then adds, "My compliments to the chef."

I smile, then reach up and run a hand over my braids, only realizing after I drop my hand that I've probably left sugary fingerprints on them. "Thank you."

"I'll definitely tell my friends about this place." He takes the change from my hand, then tips an imaginary hat at me as he backs away and heads for the door.

"Corny, but cute," I mumble, grinning and tapping a pen against the register as I watch him leave.

"He *was* cute."

I jump so high I crack my knee against the edge of the

counter. "Are you freaking Black Ops, Mom? How on earth do you *do* that?"

"Language," Mom warns, before adding, "I'm just saying, he's very attractive. You haven't gone on a date in ages. You should—"

"Put a bell around your neck so you can't sneak up on me anymore?" I rub my knee to distract myself from the pain.

"You should wear something nice when you work up front. You never know who might come in." She pauses long enough to give me what she thinks is a discreet side-eye. "And maybe, do something a little different with your hair." Mom flutters her fingers near my head as though she's casting a spell, before heading through the swinging doors to the kitchen. When she returns she's got her purse on her shoulder. "I have some errands to run. You lock up, okay?" she says before muttering something about how nice I'd look with a few curls.

"My hair is fine," I call out after her, but she's already out the door. I hop off the stool and head back to the office and the freezer whines as I walk past. "Not today, Satan, not today," I growl, determined not to let the freezer, or my Mom's hair advice, mess with my good mood.

"I didn't know you were still here," I say, entering the office just as Cassie is walking out.

"I was on my way out, but the mail just got here. I thought I'd drop it on your desk before I left." She tilts her head toward the desk. "And I straightened up a bit."

I lower myself into dad's old office chair, the rusty springs protesting when I sit. "You didn't have to do that," I say, flipping through the piles of envelopes, hoping for once to find a check somewhere in the stack.

"It was one of the things I did for your dad while you

were away. He appreciated it, and I really don't mind doing it."

I look up at Cassie. Her face is sad, and I'm reminded that I'm not the only one who misses my father. "I know Dad appreciated everything you did for him. Mom and I do, too."

She nods, but doesn't speak. I try to lighten the mood with a topic change. "You've only got a couple semesters of school left, right? Got anything lined up?"

"I'm hoping to get into a retail management position somewhere. Maybe even restaurant management. I've learned a lot working here, and I've got a lot of great ideas."

"That's awesome, Cass. If you ever need any advice or help, just let me know."

"Maybe we can talk about Cecelia's future. I really think we should update the menu."

"I'm willing to try a few things, but people love Dad's recipes, Cass. I'd hate to mess with the thing that brings so many people here, you know?"

She shrugs. "I think we're missing out on an opportunity, but it's your call, right?" Cassie's smiling, but there's tension at the edge of that smile, and I wonder if my dad's absence has affected her more than I'd considered. "Well, I'll see you Monday," she says, putting her headphones on and walking out.

I've been working on the bills for about half an hour when a knock gets my attention. I look up and see Iris leaning against the doorframe.

"Did I get our plans wrong? I thought I was meeting you later for tennis then dinner."

Iris walks into the office and flops onto the old couch across from the desk, sighing as she slips off her heels and tucks her feet under her. "Rough day at the office, so I decided I'd cut out early and grab lunch here with you."

"Patty and a cocoa bread coming up," I say, going into the kitchen and returning with Iris's favorite lunchtime meal.

"You wouldn't believe the day I've had." She takes a bite then brushes away the flaky, golden crumbs that have fallen on her blouse.

"Well, this will cheer you up," I plop down on the couch next to her. "Looks like last night is already working."

"Really?"

"We got a great write-up in today's *Post*. Plus, I've got the Chamber of Commerce meeting coming up. Between that, the mentoring program gig at the college, and the deal with Solstice, we should have no trouble making the next few month's rent."

Iris untucks her legs and closes her eyes. "Free—"

"There's a guy up front who says he needs to talk to you," Anthony interrupts, poking his head into the office.

"Did he say what about?" I ask.

"No, but he looks like he's here to stir up trouble with the stick he has up his butt."

"I better go see what this is about. What were you going to tell me?" I ask, turning to Iris once Anthony's left.

She hops off the couch and starts walking with me. "It'll keep."

When I get to the front of the restaurant there's a man standing there whose short-sleeved plaid shirt is so starched, when he turns, the shirt seems as if it's on a three-second delay.

"Hi, I'm Free, how can I help you?" I extend my hand and the man glances down at it.

"I'm Jack Nelson. With the county health department."

He speaks in short, abrupt sentences and ignores my outstretched hand.

"The county health department?"

"That's correct. I'm here as a result of a complaint we received about your restaurant."

CHAPTER TEN

The man looks at me over the top of his wire-rimmed frames before consulting the electronic tablet tucked under his arm. "We've received complaints about food not being stored at the proper temperature, food being prepared off-site in a non-registered facility then brought onto the premises, and hairnets not being worn during food preparation." He flicks his gaze up to my hair. Hair that's been hairnet-less since I'd removed it when I went back into the office.

In all the years Cecelia's been in business, we've never had a complaint called in to the health department. Dad was a stickler about keeping everything sanitary.

"Did someone get sick as a result of eating here?" Iris asks, walking up next to me.

Mr. Nelson peers at his tablet. "The complaint didn't say anything about illness."

"Well, I can't imagine why any of our customers would think something was wrong, or if they did, why they wouldn't approach us first."

"Nevertheless, we have to take every complaint seriously. I'll need access to your kitchen."

"Now?"

"Right now."

"But we weren't expecting . . ." I stop talking as Jack Nelson's lips part in an expression that looks less like a smile and more like gas pains.

"Well, that's the point of a surprise inspection isn't it, Ms. Spalding? Now, if you would lead me back to the kitchen I can get this started."

When we enter the kitchen, I shoot a pleading glance at the freezer, apologizing for my harsh words earlier and begging it to be silent for the next few minutes.

Iris, who's run ahead of us, has closed the office door. The door sticks a bit, so it's never truly closed, but she pulls it up enough so Nelson won't be able to see the mess that is my desk. I throw Iris an eyebrow *thank you* and she crosses her fingers.

We stand behind Mr. Nelson as he checks the counters, then the prep stations. He opens our refrigerator and produces his thermometer, randomly testing various items.

"Is any food prepared off premises?"

"No, all our food prep, cooking, and baking is done here onsite."

He nods and walks over to the freezer. The fist squeezing my chest tightens with each step he takes.

Mr. Nelson adjusts his glasses. "Humph, didn't know anyone still had this model."

Anthony comes over, and he, Iris, and I stand with our backs against the prep counter and wait.

Mr. Nelson opens the freezer and checks inside, performing the same thermometer checks he did on the refrigerator. After he is satisfied with inspecting the interior, he gets on his hands and knees and inspects the base and under the unit, tapping away on his tablet after each inspection.

Finally, he washes his hands at the sink then dries them on a paper towel. When he removes his glasses and starts cleaning the lenses, I begin a series of silent negotiations with God about the things I'll do if he'll keep the freezer quiet for a few minutes longer. I promise to go to church more often and to donate more to charity. I'm about to promise to be more patient with Mom when Nelson replaces his glasses and clears his throat. When he finally looks up at us, he blinks as if he's surprised to see us still standing there.

"Well, everything seems to be in order," he says.

The sigh that escapes me is cut short when Nelson adds, "For now. However, I will be following up on the visit sometime in the near future. If at that time I find any of the initial complaints warranted, you will be cited, and the citation will be reflected in your health inspection score. Do you understand?" I nod my understanding.

When he leaves, Iris and I head back to the office. "I'm going to have to replace the freezer now. Like, right now," I groan, collapsing onto the couch and hanging my head over the side of it. "I can't take the risk it's not working when he returns. The last thing we need is a failed inspection. I'll have to take the money from the Solstice gig."

"Free—"

"I mean I wasn't expecting to have to do it so soon, but . . ."

I trail off. I can tell something's up with Iris. "What?" I ask, sitting upright.

"You have to promise not to freak out, okay? I left work

early today because I was furious with Garrett."

Iris went back to New York after high school, completing her undergraduate studies and spending a year working as an admin at a small event planning company. When she surprised us all by moving back to Pointe Hill, Garrett hired her on as his assistant at Solstice, and she'd worked her way up to be one of his most trusted event planners. He's her mentor and friend, and she loves him. If she's furious with him, it could only be about one thing. "Garrett? Why?"

Iris starts pacing in the tiny space between my desk and the couch. "He's leaving the decision about the catering contract up to Simone and she's . . ." Iris comes to a stop in front of me. "I'm sorry, but Cecelia's didn't get the Solstice contract."

IRIS SITS ON THE COUCH NEXT TO ME. "I SPENT MOST OF the morning trying to get Garrett to see that giving you the contract would be great PR for Solstice, but he just wouldn't budge. He feels as though he has to give Simone some autonomy before he turns the business over to her, and this project happens to be her first major decision."

"But you said it was a done deal."

"I thought it was. This shift might have something to do with what went down last night at the CHI event."

"Do you think Christopher went to Garrett or Simone, pressured them somehow?"

"I don't know, but apparently last night's event was the first of several Solstice will be handling for CHI over the next few months. Simone's taken on a slew of new responsibilities and I think she feels like she can't afford to rock the boat."

"You almost sound like you're defending her."

"Defending her? I don't even like her. And for the record, she *reamed* me for bringing you to the event. So no, I'm definitely *not* defending her."

"I know, I'm sorry. It's not your fault. But I bet I know whose it is."

"Christopher?"

"Has to be," I say, getting up from the couch. "Solstice, the inspection. I mentioned the trouble with the freezer when I went to his office."

"You think he called in the complaint?"

"The great Christopher Bellamy do his own grunt work? No, he probably got one of his minions to do it for him."

"But the event was just last night."

"If you'd seen his office, you'd know he's connected enough to get what he wants when he wants it." I lean against the desk. "And to think, I was actually feeling sorry for him."

"Why would you ever feel sorry for *him*?" Iris asks.

I cradle my head in my hands. "Mom told me he came by the house the morning after prom."

I wait for Iris's reaction, but when none comes I look up. Her face is a mix of uncertainty and regret. "You knew. You knew Christopher came to see me that morning and you never told me?"

Iris stares down at her feet and shakes her head.

"Iris?"

When she finally looks up, the expression on her face is all the confirmation I need. "How could you keep that from me? You knew how devastated I was that morning. How I cried myself to sleep for weeks after."

"I know, I know, Free, and I'm sorry. Part of me wanted to tell you, I swear, but I promised your parents I wouldn't."

"And the other part of you? What did the other part of you want?"

Iris hesitates momentarily, then says, "The other part of me wanted you to face the facts. Christopher humiliated you in front of our entire senior class, and nothing he could have said that morning would have changed that. If keeping him away from you was the only way to get you to see that, then it was a decision I was willing to make. I hope you can understand, Free."

"The only thing I understand, is you've been lying to me for seven years. And you know what? It makes me wonder what else you've been lying to me about."

CHAPTER ELEVEN

I close the office door, in case Cassie and Anthony are still mulling around out front, then look at Iris.

"I haven't lied to you about anything, Free," Iris says.

"Except this, you mean. How could you do this? Christopher being a part of my life—or not—wasn't anyone's decision to make but mine."

"I know, but the first time he left, you were so broken by it we were afraid for you. What if he'd apologized then just lied to you again?"

"But now I'll never know what would have happened." I drop down onto the couch. "We were going to go away together."

Iris sits beside me. "You never told me that."

"We didn't tell anybody. If my parents had found out, they'd have shipped me off to Jamaica in the middle of the night."

"When did you plan all this?"

"We had talked about it all through junior year, but when he went away that summer I thought it was all over.

When we reconnected at the end of senior year, though, it was like we picked up as if we'd never been apart."

"What about college? What about everything you'd said you wanted to do."

"I would have done those things. We were going to spend the summer after senior year traveling Europe. We'd both gotten in to Brandton University, and Christopher was getting a monthly allowance from his father that would have covered an apartment off campus."

"Why didn't you tell me any of this?"

"Because you and I barely spent any time together senior year. You were going up to New York almost every weekend. You weren't even here on prom night, Iris."

"That's not fair. You pulled away from me, too. And you knew I'd always planned on going back up to my old school for their prom. But when Christopher backed out on you, I invited you to come with me and my friends."

"I know," I say, fiddling with the frayed material on the couch's arm. "But I didn't want your pity. I didn't want you inviting me because you felt sorry for me."

Iris takes me by the shoulders and turns me to face her. "I invited you because you're my cousin and I love you, and I wanted you to have an amazing prom." She starts to say something else, but stops.

"Say it."

"Honestly, Free, I can't believe you even agreed to go to the prom with him in the first place. He just up and left the summer after junior year. You went months without a word from him. You didn't even know he was back in town until you heard people talking about it at school."

I open my mouth, wanting to defend myself, but can't find the right words.

"Do you remember how distraught you were when you called me on prom night?" she asks.

"*Remember*? Of course I remember. I'm the one who stood there like a fool and watched Christopher walk into the gym with Jessica on his arm." I stand and begin pacing in front of the couch. "His mom was still recovering from the car accident she and Jason had been in a few weeks prior, so when he told me he wouldn't be going to the prom, I understood. I knew he was going through a lot, so I didn't press it. I went with friends instead."

"But why did you even agree to go see him in the first place? Why after he'd been gone so long, did you just fall right back into his arms?"

"I know what it looked like to everyone else, but the night of the accident when Christopher called, I knew he needed me."

"Well, he got you."

I stop pacing and look at her. The pain must be evident in my face, because she says softly, "I know Christopher's type, Free. I *was* the type. When you can't be with the one you want, you'll settle for being with the one who wants you. He used you."

I shake my head. "You didn't hear him that night. He was sobbing so hard when he called I could barely make out what he was saying. He didn't know whether his mother would make it or not. His father was in London, and he was alone."

I search Iris's eyes to see if she understands. She nods, and I continue. "I know it sounds stupid, but there's a connection between us, and even through the time and distance, I felt it. When we were together that night it was like we were repairing that connection."

"How strong could that connection have been if he

showed up at the prom with Jessica after telling you he wasn't going? Did he think you'd change your mind about going, or that you wouldn't find out? Whatever his reasoning, he was a jerk for treating you that way."

The pity in Iris's voice hurts as much as the truth in her words. Tears burn the back of my eyes, and I pinch the bridge of my nose to prevent them from falling. I don't want to talk about that night anymore. I don't want to talk about prom, and I certainly don't want Iris's pity. I walk around to the file cabinet and open it. "The point is you should have told me Christopher had come by the house."

Iris walks over to the desk. "You're right, Free, and I'm sorry I kept it from you. I would never do anything like that again. I know we drifted apart when we went away to school. But I missed you, and I'm glad you're back."

"I missed you, too."

I'm about to walk around the desk to give her a hug when she adds, "Just be careful with Christopher, okay? He hadn't earned the right to ask you for forgiveness back then, and he doesn't deserve a minute of your sympathy now."

"I know how to handle myself around Christopher."

Iris pauses then says, "I've heard those words before, Free."

I don't know if it's the pity in her eyes or the certainty in her words, but suddenly, I'm too overwhelmed to look at her. I push the file drawer to shut it, but the overstuffed drawer doesn't close all the way, robbing me of the satisfying slam of metal striking metal. "You've made your opinion pretty clear, Iris. Of Christopher and of me."

She doesn't move, and I know one of us should say something, should suggest we go out for drinks to hammer this out, but neither of us do.

"I have a lot of work to do," I say, opening another

drawer and trying to read the words on a folder through my blurred vision. A tear falls onto the folder, and I hold my breath to stifle a sniffle. Finally, I hear the door creak, and when I turn, Iris is gone, leaving me alone with a pile of bills and a sick feeling in the pit of my stomach.

CHAPTER TWELVE

It's been about two weeks since my fight with Iris and we haven't spoken much. We've exchanged a few texts, and she's been by the restaurant a couple of times, but we haven't talked about what went down between us, and I'm not sure I'm ready to.

But business is good, and Mom, maybe because she senses something going on with Iris and me, has been really sweet. She's still not happy I signed the lease, but she hasn't brought it up again. As an apology, I get to the restaurant early to make her a special breakfast.

"Did you make fritters?" she asks, as she walks through the back door and joins me at the stove.

I place the last golden brown fritter onto a plate. "I know how much you love them, and I realized I hadn't made you any since I've been back."

Mom stares wistfully at the fritters. "They were your dad's favorite, too."

"I know." I turn off the burner and take the platter to the counter, patting a stool to let her know it's time to sit.

She sits, watching as I set a place at the counter with

two plates, cloth napkins, and silverware. I pull up a stool next to her, and I'm about to start eating when I notice she hasn't even picked up her fork. "What's wrong?"

She smiles and shakes her head. "I just can't remember the last time someone made me breakfast."

I lower my fork. Daddy used to make her breakfast every morning. I've been back almost a year and every time I feel like I understand the depth of my mother's loss, something happens to remind me how integral my parents were in each other's lives. I look at my mom's plate and my heart breaks for her all over again.

She picks up her fork, cuts off a piece and blows on it before putting into her mouth. All of a sudden, I'm ten years old again, standing over her at my homemade Mother's Day breakfast, waiting for her smile of approval.

Mom chews slowly, then a smile blossoms on her face. "As good as I remember," she says.

I squeeze her hand. "I had amazing teachers." I bite right into a fritter even though I know it's still too hot.

Mom chuckles. "Your father used to do that all the time." She shakes her head. "You're so much like him. He loved my fritters, you know. Told me they were better than your Grandma Cecelia's. He always said it in a whisper, though, like he was afraid she'd hear him even from the grave." She stares at her plate for a while.

"Who taught you how to make them?" I ask softly.

"My grandmother, Linda. I was maybe eleven, twelve. Back then in Jamaica, we'd cook over an open flame in the backyard. She'd sit on a low wooden stool and spend the better part of the day out there prepping and cooking breadfruit, green bananas, plantains. But fritters were her favorite." She pats my knee. "Thank you, Free. These are as good as your dad's."

The compliment brings tears to my eyes. "Dad always made his fritters so big, though," I say, and Mom and I both laugh through our sniffling.

"He wanted to make sure people got a lot for their money. He knew how hard they worked, and he wanted them to know their hard earned dollars would always go far here." Mom looks around the kitchen, and we sit in silence, holding hands while we finish breakfast. When Cassie and Anthony join us later, I serve them the remaining fritters, and the four of us eat and reminisce about my father until it's time to open up.

We're busy throughout the day, and Cassie and Anthony stay late into the evening to help me prep for the next day. When I go to the front of the restaurant to close the register, Cassie follows and leans against the counter as she watches me. "Anthony told me about what happened with Solstice," she says.

"Apparently, since our menu doesn't include words like *artisanal*, *foraged*, or *deconstructed*, we're not worth Simone's time."

She shrugs. "She might have a point. Things are changing around here, Free. You were gone for a long time, and the neighborhood isn't what it was when you left."

"We're still doing good business, and our main dishes are still popular."

"For how long, though? I just think either we go with the flow, or we end up drowning." She leans closer. "Mr. Spalding and I were talking about a new menu before he, well . . . he was starting to see it was time for something different. There are tons of new people moving into the neighborhood who would appreciate something a bit more elegant."

"Dad wanted to change the menu?"

"He was thinking about it. I shared some ideas with him, even showed him the Island Shack menu."

Cassie's revelation stuns me. Daddy had always said he would only serve "real food" at Cecelia's. That these fusion-type restaurants missed the point of giving people an authentic Jamaican experience.

"I'm sorry, Free. I didn't mean to . . ." Cassie trails, then picks up with another thought. "I loved your dad, and I love this restaurant. I just want what's best for it."

Cassie wraps an arm around my shoulder and I lean into her. "I know."

She starts to say something else, but Anthony walks up and motions for me to join him in the kitchen.

"The mentoring program's coordinator left me a message to call him," he says, once we're in the kitchen. Anthony returns the call and places the phone on speaker when he gets Craig, the coordinator, on the line. I listen as Craig explains that the college has postponed the mentoring program's launch. A postponement that means no catering contract for Cecelia's. At least not any time soon.

"University-level bureaucracy" is how the coordinator explains it. When Anthony ends the call, I say, "A five- to six-month delay? We don't have that kind of time. We needed that gig yesterday."

"Yeah, but like Craig said, the program needs computer equipment, software, businesses to volunteer to mentor the students. It can't launch without those things."

"You know what this is, right? A few months ago, all the program needed was a couple of signatures, and now it's being delayed for months? This has Christopher written all over it. He thinks if he can delay the program long enough, I'll be forced to give up my lease. I'm one of the last holdouts. If I go, I bet he thinks the rest will quickly follow suit." I thread my fingers together, resting my hands on my head and chewing on the inside of my cheek.

"I know that look," Anthony says. "The last time I saw it, you were on your way to C. J. Eubanks's office. I don't think—"

"Tell Mom I left to run errands. Don't worry about coming in early tomorrow, just finish prepping for the morning. I'll owe you one." I grab my keys then dig through my purse as I head to the parking lot.

Inside my parents' old pickup truck, I inhale a long, slow breath through my nose and stare at the business card in my hand. On the exhale, I punch Christopher's number into my phone. He picks up on the first ring.

"Eubanks," he barks, sounding like a drill instructor.

"Is this a game to you?" I ask.

"Excuse me?"

"You sent the inspector to Cecelia's, and you made sure I was out of the running with the Solstice gig. Now you've somehow gotten to the college, too. Understand something, Christopher, my life, my restaurant, *my livelihood*, are not pieces on a chessboard you can move around like you're some kind of king. This is *not* a game."

After a few seconds of silence, he says, "I don't play games."

"Not fair, anyway."

"I'm busy. Unless you're calling to tell me to rip up the lease, I don't have time for this."

Insufferable prick. "We need to talk. Now."

Christopher hesitates before saying, "Now's not a good time for me."

"Lucky for me I don't care what's good for you. If you think I made a stink at your little event the other night, you're not ready for the load I'm about to dump at your door."

Christopher barks out an expletive, then, "Meet me at twenty-five Westview in fifteen minutes. It's a few blocks down from The Depot."

It's my turn to hesitate.

"I'm not at the office," he says in response to my silence. "If you want to meet me today, that's where I'll be." Then the line goes dead.

"Son of a . . ." I bang the phone against the steering wheel.

Christopher Bellamy's selfishness messed up my past, there's no way I'm going to let him mess up my future. I start the engine, check my rearview mirror, then ease the truck into traffic, hoping I figure out the rules to Christopher's game before it's too late.

FIFTEEN MINUTES LATER I SWING THE TRUCK INTO THE gravel driveway of a mid-century bungalow. The dumpster in the yard and the bobcat in the driveway suggest the old house is about to become another one of Pointe Hill's casualties. But there are no workers around, and the only car in the driveway is a luxury sedan that looks out of place on a block lined with cars as old as my parents' truck.

I peep up at the house through the windshield, annoyed Christopher isn't outside waiting for me, then jump out and head up the front steps onto the porch. The wood on the wraparound porch is worn; the once burgundy paint, a dusty, faded brown. An old, rusty swing hangs from the porch's rafters, and it squeaks as it sways in the breeze. I bang my fist on the screen door and look inside.

"Hello?" Nothing. I open the screen door and call out again. "Christopher, it's Free." When there's still no answer, I stick my head inside.

The hardwood floors are scratched and broken in some places. The wooden bannister leading upstairs is missing several rails. A faint smell of mildew fills the air. I release the screen door, letting it slap close behind me, and venture into the small foyer. I call out again but get no response. There's a fireplace in the living room, and light reflecting off something on the mantel catches my eye. After taking another look around, I walk to the fireplace and study the faded photo in the small, silver frame.

A woman and two boys are seated on a couch. Both boys share the woman's features; dark hair that curls around their ears, square jaws. But only the older boy has her brown eyes. The younger boy's eyes are green, vivid even in the dark, grainy picture. Despite the presence of a cake on the table in front of them, no one in the picture is smiling.

I pick up the frame and wipe the grime away with my thumb. Only then do I see a man sitting on the opposite end of the couch, face turned away from the camera, arm draped across the back.

"That's the only picture I have of the four of us together," Christopher says.

I jump, fumbling the picture in my hands. Christopher catches it before it falls.

"I didn't mean to . . ."

He doesn't respond, instead, he cradles the picture frame as though it was made of eggshells.

"One of the guys from the crew that's gonna demo the place found a bunch of boxes in the attic. This was in one of them."

I look around and see a pair of dingy curtains hanging

from the window, an old couch pushed up against a wall. The same couch in the picture.

I stare wide-eyed at Christopher. "This was where you lived." My mind flashes to the dumpster in the front yard. "You're tearing it down?"

"*Lived* is being generous, but yeah. And yes, it's scheduled to be torn down in a few weeks. The only memories I have worth saving didn't happen here." He returns the frame to the mantel.

When I met Christopher in the tenth grade, he'd just moved to Pointe Hill. Like me, he'd sought refuge in the school library. Unlike me, he could probably have hung out with just about anyone. So it turned more than a few heads when he chose me. We were inseparable until he went to live with his dad the summer after our junior year. But in all the years he lived in Pointe Hill, I'd never once been to his house. I'd wanted to come over, wanted to meet his mother, but both had remained off-limits.

I asked him why once, and he'd said, "*I* don't even want to be there, why would I ever want to take you there?" I never brought it up again.

I study him as he studies the picture. The suit and tie are gone. His hair is damp and sticking up in places. The once white T-shirt he's wearing stretches taut across his shoulders, the thread frayed around a hole at the seam. This is the Christopher I remember. Intense and imperfect. Guarded yet transparent.

"Whenever we talked on the phone back then, I'd close my eyes and imagine you in your bedroom. I pictured a typical guy's room, or at least what I thought one looked like. Beige walls and brown carpet, a pile of dirty laundry on your floor. I'd always picture you lying on your back in bed." I press my hand against my stomach. "And your hand would be on your stomach the way it always was whenever you were deep in thought." I smile and gesture to where his hand currently rests just above his belt.

The memory is so vivid, I can almost hear him breathing on the other end of the line as we both drifted in and out of sleep, exhausted but unwilling to sever the connection.

Christopher chuckles. "My thoughts of you in your bedroom were a little less . . . PG."

He looks at me, and all I see is the eleventh-grade, on-the-phone-with-me-until-dawn Christopher, and the old connection between us sparks like electricity. But I tear my eyes away, because electricity is the last thing I need when I feel like I'm neck deep in rising water.

"How is she?" I ask, nodding toward the picture on the mantel.

The abrupt shift in conversation seems to catch Christopher off guard, but he answers. "She's okay. She has good days and bad." He pauses before adding, "I haven't been to see her in a while."

The car accident that brought Christopher back into my life left Ms. Bellamy with a head injury that would require lifelong care. It also ended Jason's college football career. Although Christopher hadn't even been in the car, the guilt he felt that night had been palpable.

I wait, wondering if he'll say more. When he doesn't, I ask, "Is that your father in the picture?"

Christopher nods. "But I don't remember him being there. I don't even remember that night. I think I was five, and we were celebrating Jason's sixth birthday. It would explain Mom bothering to get dressed that day."

Even before the accident, we all knew something wasn't right with Ms. Bellamy. The few times she'd shown up at school for parent teacher conferences, the slurred speech and glassy eyes had been a dead giveaway. And whenever Christopher came by the restaurant, my mom would watch him scarf down food and wearily say, "They're not feeding that boy right." But I had no idea her demons had been a part of her sons' lives as far back as the picture indicated. I rest my hand on Christopher's.

He looks at my hand, then into my eyes. "I wanted to," he says.

"Wanted to what?"

He clears his throat and continues. "Wanted to invite you over. Once, when Mom was away, I came close. I wanted to cook you dinner. It wouldn't have been anything like your dad cooked, just pasta, but . . ." He trails off.

"Why didn't you?" I ask on behalf of the sixteen-year-old me who would have loved nothing better than to have Christopher cook dinner for her.

He stares at me. He's opening a door he'd never opened to me before and I want to hear more. I tighten my grip on his hand and ask again. "Why didn't you?"

"My family was nothing like yours. My life in this house wasn't something I wanted you to see." Then he breaks off the thought and picks up a new one. "You really didn't know I came to your house the morning after prom?"

It's his turn to surprise me with a topic change. "My mom only told me a few days ago," I say.

"I came to try to explain what happened. How it happened. Free, I didn't know you'd be there. I would never have done that to you. I meant everything I said that night we were together, but there were things that weren't in my control. I—"

My cell phone vibrates in my pocket and in the almost

empty room the buzzing might as well be a bullhorn. I try to ignore it, but it gets louder with each vibration.

"You should get that," Christopher says, letting my hand fall away from his as he steps back.

I grab my phone from my back pocket and step into the foyer.

"Hello?"

"The freezer just quit on us," Anthony says.

The pull back to reality is like having a bucket of ice water dumped on my head, washing away the moment I've just shared with Christopher. "Are you sure it really quit? Sometimes it does that thing where—"

"It's done. I was putting some things away before leaving, and I realized it was quiet. Like dead quiet. I guess we could try to get the repair guy out here to look at it, but that would be the third time in as many months. We can't keep putting bandages on it. Danielle said—"

"Who's Danielle?"

"The girl I was talking to at the restaurant the day after the CHI event. We were going to go out later and she came here first. Anyway, her dad knows someone who sells restaurant equipment, and long story short, he can get us a really good deal on a closeout model."

"How much?"

Anthony rattles off a number that is probably less than it could be but more than my mind can currently wrap around. I'll have to put it on my personal credit card. Thank God for good credit. I keep my body still, not wanting to tip Christopher off that I've just entered full-fledged crisis mode.

"There's more," Anthony says.

"Please tell me it's good more and not bad more."

"A little of both. The good more is that Mr. Makao

already took some of the stuff from the freezer back to store at his restaurant. The Fosters took a bunch, too, and they said they could keep it there as long as we need to."

"And the bad?"

"Earlier, Aunt Agnes saw the inspector down the street. He went into the Italian restaurant, and she locked up before she saw whether he was coming here or not, but . . ."

"But we can't take the chance he comes back tomorrow and we don't have a working freezer." I turn to look at Christopher. He's standing in front of the fireplace, hands in his pockets, head tilted, eyeing me with curiosity. The head tilt, the hands in the pocket, they were the kind of things that had my high school heart falling hard for him. The things that had everyone falling for him. But as I listen to Anthony explain what a good deal he's managed to wrangle for the freezer, all I can see is the man who's doing a great job of screwing up my life right now.

"The guy says he can get the freezer to us this evening if we want it, but we have to do it now. It's the last one he's got in stock. Aunt Agnes was already gone by the time I realized the freezer was done for it, so I called you first. Should I call her, too?"

"No, don't call her. I'll be there soon." The last thing I need is another round of *I told you so* from my mother.

"Oh, and Free, you do remember we only have three days until the chamber meeting, right?"

"Damn," I say under my breath. I'd planned on driving up to Atlanta when I left the restaurant earlier to get the ingredients I'd need for the menu I was planning, but my visit to Christopher nixed that.

"I'll stay tonight until everything gets set up, and I can come in the morning, too," Anthony says.

"I don't know what I would do without you, Anthony," I

say, loud enough for Christopher to hear. I watch as his expression teeters between curiosity and annoyance.

"Neither do I," Anthony says, chuckling then disconnecting the call.

"Me too," I say to the dead air on the other end of the line as I watch Christopher. At those last words, Christopher's expression hardens and he heads toward the front door.

"Sounds like you're wanted elsewhere," he says, throwing open the screen door.

"I came here to ask you to fight fair," I glance over my shoulder at the picture on the mantel and shove the phone back in my pocket. "And for a minute I thought maybe I'd caught a glimpse of the old Christopher."

"That picture," he says tilting his head toward the mantel, "is the closest thing you'll get to the old Christopher. And as for fighting fair, all is fair in love and war, isn't that what they say?"

I stand in the doorway facing him. In the narrow space, I'm forced to look up to meet his eyes. The porch light throws hard, unwavering shadows across his face. "So, this is war?" I ask.

Chris's gaze sweeps over my face. "Well, it sure as hell isn't love."

It hasn't been love between us for a long time, but it still hurts to hear him say it. I walk through the door and to my car. The last thing I hear as the rocks slip out from under my tire as I peel out of the driveway is the screen door slapping shut.

CHAPTER THIRTEEN

I drive back to the restaurant with my music up and the windows down. The muggy night air stings my eyes and whips my hair against my face, but no amount of warm air and thumping beats can erase the sting of Christopher's words. I'm halfway to the restaurant when Anthony calls to tell me the freezer will be delivered soon.

"You sound tired," he tells me. "Go home. Cass and I'll take care of it."

I end the call, blinking back the exhaustion weighing down my eyelids, then make a sharp right toward my apartment complex. But I drive past my apartment, past the new construction and old houses that dot Pointe Hill's landscape like pieces on a checkerboard. Past the park where the whirring buzz of tree crickets and cicadas compete with the music coming from my truck's speakers, and before I know it, I'm at the restaurant unlocking the front door.

Voices drift from the kitchen, but I linger up front. The dining area is dark except for the street lamp filtering gauzy strips of light in through the half-open blinds. I run my fingers along the rough edges of the tables and chairs as I walk through and close the blinds, then I sit at my favorite booth. It's the one in the far corner, and it's perfect for people watching.

The last diners left hours ago, but I can almost hear their silverware clinking against their plates, feel the crackle of laughter as they carry on conversations above the steel drums playing through the speakers. The smell of onions and fried sprat—the day's special—still permeates the air, and mixes with the scent of sugar buns and the fresh coconut we grated for the rice and peas.

I run my hand under the edge of the table, stopping when I reach the gouge in the wood and tracing the letters with my fingers: FS. When I was still too young to help in the kitchen, this booth was where Mom sat me to fold napkins and fill salt and pepper shakers. One afternoon after we'd closed, I carved my initials under the table. Mom walked up just as I popped my head up.

"What did you do?" she asked, her eyebrows knitted.

By the time she slid into the booth and started feeling around under the table, I was running the list of potential punishments through my seven-year-old mind.

Now, I move my fingers and trace the letters "AS," then move them to the right and trace the "RS." Mom had etched her initials next to mine. Later, Daddy etched his there, too.

The memory does what the car ride here didn't. It clears away the fog that descends whenever I think about my past with Christopher. It reminds me that Cecelia's isn't just my parents' place, it's mine. The fighting with Christopher, the battles with mom, aren't just about my past; they are about my future.

Earlier, Anthony told me to go home, but Cecelia's *is* home and has been for as long as I can remember. I don't know what I'd do without it, and I'm determined not to find out. I run my fingers along the carvings one last time, then head to the kitchen, jingling my keys to announce my entrance.

"This is my first up-close-and-personal with a real chef," a girl says to Anthony as I enter. I recognize her from her mass of wild curly hair as the girl I'd teased Anthony about before.

"I'm glad I could be your first," Anthony answers.

"Dude, your game sucks," Cassie says, from the other end of the kitchen where she's working at the smaller prep station.

The girl emits a loud snort-laugh that makes me chuckle. She looks up when I enter, but Anthony doesn't, even when I laugh. I toss my keys on the counter. Anthony turns toward me and I see why he didn't hear me come in. He's not wearing his hearing aid.

"Fancy knife-work," I say, pointing at the mound of perfectly diced vegetables on the cutting board in front of him.

Anthony looks at me sheepishly. "Yeah . . . I figured I might as well get some prepping done while I waited for the delivery." He wipes his hands on his apron. "Free, this is Danielle. We have a couple classes together at Pointe State."

"Hi," Danielle says, extending a hand and flashing a smile straight out of a toothpaste ad. "I've heard a lot about you."

"About what a pain in the ass I am?" I tease, shaking her hand. Danielle's dressed in a pair of pants and a frilly top, both of which look more like they've come off a runway than a rack.

She laughs. "He said he doesn't know what he'd do without you."

I look at Anthony, who's studiously avoiding eye

contact, and gently shoulder-check him. "The feeling is mutual. He's one of the good ones."

"Free," Anthony groans.

I let him off the hook and walk over to Cassie. "Thanks for staying, Cass."

She shrugs. "Anthony stayed, and I didn't have other plans." She peeks over at Danielle and Anthony. "Plus," she says louder, "someone had to do some actual work instead of putting on a piece of performance art." Anthony grins, and Danielle and I stifle our laughter.

I brush a few strands of hair off Cassie's forehead so I can see her eyes. Despite the levity of the previous moment, she seems sad. "You and I haven't hung out in a while. Want to catch a movie when things slow down a bit? My treat."

"That new rom-com looks *really* good," she says, a sly grin spreading across her face. I hate rom-coms and their cheesy endings, and she knows it, but I say yes anyway.

"You'll love it," she calls out as I head back to the office.

Anthony follows me. "Freezer should be here any time now," he says once we're in the office. "The Makaos and the Fosters really stepped up, you know."

"I know. We could have had a lot of food go bad if they hadn't stored it for us. We have to thank them." The minute I say it, an idea takes shape in my head. "Tomorrow evening, I'll invite them here for dinner."

"I could just bring them lunch tomorrow."

"You could, but I want them here, sitting in the booths and reminiscing about the times they had when Dad was still here. He used to have them and their children over for game night once a month. I want to start doing that again. I want to remind them what it feels like to be part of a community."

Anthony grins. "And?"

"Well," I say, dragging the word out as I rock back on the old squeaky chair and prop my feet up. "If a few of them have second thoughts about letting their leases expire, that would just be a bonus, wouldn't it?"

Cassie taps on the office door, then pops her head in. "The freezer's here."

I rifle through a stack of envelopes on my desk. "Did you find the credit card?"

"Cassie did, but only after we'd dug around that desk forever. It's a mess," Anthony says.

"Luckily, Cassie makes a great assistant," I say.

I mean it as a compliment, but the expression on Cassie's face tells me she doesn't see it that way. She turns to Anthony. "You coming?"

"Right behind you," he answers.

When Cassie leaves, I say, "Does she seem okay to you? Lately she seems a little, I don't know . . . distant."

He shrugs. "No more than usual. She's always willing to pitch in whenever I need her."

I sigh. "You do know she's crazy about you, right?"

"What?"

"Guys," I say, shaking my head as I walk past him, "can't see what's right in front of their own faces. We'll talk about it later. Now let's go see a man about a freezer."

CHAPTER FOURTEEN

The guys have the new freezer installed and up and running in no time. They load the old freezer into the back of their truck, and I stand on the sidewalk watching as another piece of my father's life rolls out of my life for good.

When I return to the kitchen, Cassie is grating coconut for the gizzada cakes and bobbing her head under her headphones. Anthony's finishing his prep work, and Danielle's in the pantry stocking supplies. After I wash my hands and don an apron, I grab a knife and a bowl of vegetables, and take a seat across from Anthony.

He looks toward the pantry then says quietly, "I hope you don't mind Danielle being here. I told her we could reschedule the date, but she said she wanted to stop by. She ended up staying to help."

"So, it *was* a date?" I ask, grinning.

"Not a *date* date, but we had plans."

"Isn't she worried about messing up that outfit? That top alone is worth more than everything I'm wearing." I tilt my head toward the pantry.

Anthony picks up a green pepper. "This pepper is probably worth more than everything you're wearing."

We both laugh, and Anthony's good mood gives me the opening I need to broach a touchy subject. I can hear the tinny sound of Cassie's music coming from her headphones, but look at her to make sure she's still wearing them. I tap my knife against the counter to get Anthony's attention, then tilt my head toward the pantry where Danielle is. "Is *she* why you're not wearing it?" I ask, pointing at my ear.

I say it quietly, but I could have just mouthed the words, because Anthony reads lips. He taught himself how when, as a kid, neither his teachers nor foster parents picked up on his hearing loss.

"Didn't feel like it," he says, through pinched lips.

He might act like he made this decision lightly, but I know better. "You shouldn't have to hide who you are from anyone."

Anthony opens his mouth to speak, but I hold up a hand to stop him. "I'm not saying who you are is that one thing," I tap my ear again, "just that it is a part of you, and if she has a problem with it—"

"She doesn't have a problem with it. I don't even think she knows. I just didn't feel like wearing it tonight. Let's not turn it into a federal case, okay?"

Anthony starts chopping again, and I study his face. Long lashes hide large, dark brown eyes, and his lips are set in a thin line. I reach over and still his hand with mine, and he looks up.

"Okay," I say. We're silent for a few beats until I ask, "Did I ever tell you how I met Christopher?"

He looks surprised. The only things he knows about Christopher are the staccato sentences he's overheard over the years. First real boyfriend. Took another girl to the prom. Broke Free's heart.

"This might come as a complete shock to you, but I was kind of a nerd in high school."

Anthony looks down at my Wonder Woman T-shirt. "You don't say."

I toss a carrot stick at him and he swats it away, laughing. "Well, imagine all this," I wave my hand with a flourish, "but shorter and with a huge afro. I didn't win any popularity contests, wasn't even invited to enter any. Pointe Hill High was money back then. Most of the kids didn't have to work, and even the ones who worked didn't work like I did. So while everyone was joining the track team, meeting at Foster's after school for ice cream, or summering in Hilton Head, I was here. Every day before and after school, and all day during the summer." The laughter that was in my voice a moment ago is gone. "It stays with you."

Anthony frowns. "What does?"

"Everything about having to be me when everyone else was out there just being teenagers. And no matter how much I tried to fit in, working here was like a stain I couldn't get rid of. The restaurant smell . . . it was like it was in my skin." I hold my hands up and study them. "My fingers would be stained yellow for days after we served curry. I thought everyone could see it. So I mostly kept to myself."

Anthony doesn't say anything. He doesn't need to. He's also chosen solitude when anything more seemed too difficult.

"I stopped going to study hall, stopped eating in the cafeteria. I went to the library instead. Did that all through junior high and freshman year of high school. I mean, I had friends, but I preferred to be by myself most of the time.

Until one day in the tenth grade, this kid walked up to my table."

"Christopher?"

I nod. "The library was practically empty, but he asked me if the seat across from me was taken, then sat down before I even answered. He and Jason were new to the school, but I knew who he was. Everyone did. They made quite a pair, those two. And Christopher's eyes." I shake my head remembering the first time I saw them up close. The color reminded me of the lush green of the painting of Hope Gardens my parents kept in the office.

"We had lunch together in the library almost every day that school year and the next. He was my best friend. That's why everything that happened was so . . ." I trail off, walking to the sink and rinsing the vegetables until the cold water starts to numb my fingers. When I return to the counter, Anthony watches me intently.

"Christopher was the first person to choose me. Mom and Dad and Iris loved me, but they were family. Christopher *chose* me. Graphic T-shirts, stained fingers, and all." I look up. "He gave me a promise necklace, a locket shaped like a book. It wasn't even real, but he had these big dreams and plans, and so did I."

"So what happened?"

I pick up the knife and start peeling. "He chose other things. Other people. First his dad, then Jessica."

"The girl he brought to the prom?"

I nod. "For the longest time after, I thought maybe if I'd been more like her, things would have been different. When I went away to college I even tried to be that girl. I dressed differently, talked differently, acted differently."

"And?"

"It worked for a while," I say, shrugging. "I dated a lot. I was really good at my job, made more friends, finally ended up in what I thought was a great relationship. But none of that turned out the way I thought it would."

"Why not?"

"Secrets. Lies. Mine and other people's." I rest my hand on Anthony's. "The one thing I learned is that you should never pretend to be someone you aren't to get someone you want."

Anthony glances over at the pantry. When he looks back I say, "If you do, it ends up hurting way more than if you never got what you wanted in the first place."

CHAPTER FIFTEEN

"They're a little . . ." Cassie pinches off a corner of a lamb patty and the crust snaps, scattering flakes of pastry across the counter.

"Dry," we say in unison.

I plop down onto a stool and stare at the small tray of cocktail patties in front of me while Cassie studies the handwritten recipe. "I don't know what we're doing wrong. Mr. Spalding and I made these together a couple of times."

I knew Cassie enjoyed baking. She'd been bringing brownies made from a mix as treats for my parents for years. But I didn't know she'd graduated to making recipes from scratch with Dad. I pick up the paper with the recipe written on it and study it. It's wrinkled, and the ink is smeared in spots where it's gotten wet. Cassie's handwriting replaces my father's in the spots where the drops have erased Dad's writing. I run my finger across the raised smudges and imagine my father writing his recipes down by hand instead of using the computer I got them for Christmas a couple of years ago.

"We'll get it right," Cassie says, laying a reassuring arm

across my shoulders.

I fold the paper along the well-worn creases then place it on the counter. "We don't have a choice. The chamber meeting is tomorrow night. I can't blow this, Cass. Yesterday I got a call from Sandra, the woman who invited me to the meeting. She told me a couple of investors are going to be there. They're looking to invest in a few businesses that have a long history in the community."

Cassie blows out a puff of air then takes the seat next to me. "Wow, that could change everything."

"If I can get just one of those investors on our side, I can help Cecelia's and these other businesses more than I ever imagined. Everything I've been through since I've been back would have been worth it. The fights with Mom, working these long hours here, even seeing Christopher again."

Cassie looks at the tray of patties. "My classes start early tomorrow, but I can stay."

I wave her off. "Go, I'll stay until I get it right."

She heads to the office and returns carrying her bag. "You'll be fine, I know you will," she says, though the look in her eyes tells me she might not be as confident as she sounds.

When she's gone, I drag another bag of flour from the pantry. As I mix a new batch of dough, I think back to yesterday evening when I invited the Makaos and the Fosters, along with some of the other Old Sixth Ward merchants, over to thank them for helping us out when our freezer died.

Anthony and I had pulled several tables together, and while our friends' children and grandchildren sat playing board games, we talked about the community and the changes taking place in Pointe Hill.

"Everything's different now," Mr. Foster had said. "They're building houses right on top of one another."

"But you have to admit, Pointe Hill needed something," Mrs. Foster had replied. "People were moving away, the houses were empty. We *needed* something."

Mr. Foster had rubbed a hand over his graying beard and continued as though he hadn't heard his wife. "Just yesterday, I heard they were tearing down that little apartment complex on Lexington and putting up two houses on the land." He'd held up two fingers to emphasize his point. "*Two houses* on land that used to be home to a dozen families. And there's nowhere for those families to go now but out of town. They can't afford anything here now."

Mr. Makao, who had been silent throughout much of dinner, had finally spoken, then. "Pretty soon none of us will be able to stay. The rent they're asking is just too much, and taxes are skyrocketing."

His comment had given me the opportunity to broach the topic I'd been wanting to all night. "I can't imagine Pointe Hill without all of you here. Mr. Makao, you make the best Thai food in town. And Mr. Foster, when I was a kid, getting a rum raisin cone after church was as right as rice and peas with Sunday dinner. I want your kids and grandkids to have that, too. I know none of you have renewed your lease, but I think you should seriously consider it. I've seen Cecelia's business pick up since I spoke at the CHI event. It's not going to be easy, and it will mean doing business in a way we're not used to, but we have to try."

Anthony had spoken up then. "Free's right. There are things we can do."

"It's a struggle for some of these folks just to pay rent," my mother had said, addressing the group for the first time that evening. "You can't expect them to be able to compete with these new businesses with their big budgets and all their twittering."

Anthony and I had chuckled, and then he'd tried to ease her fears. "It's called tweeting, Auntie. And marketing doesn't have to be expensive. I've got friends in my classes who are studying advertising, others want to become web developers and graphic designers. They need internships and work experience."

"I think I've come up with a way we can all help each other," I'd said, then shared my ideas for helping the original Old Sixth Ward merchants hold their own among the new businesses.

They were skeptical, but before they'd left I'd hobbled together an outline to present at tomorrow's chamber meeting, and everyone in attendance had agreed to support me as head of the chamber's special committee. They had also assured me they would talk to the other businesses, and I had promised them they could trust me to take the lead on this project because I would be able to get things done. I look down at the tray of burned patties and sigh. These people are trusting me with their futures, and I can't even get a simple recipe right.

I'm still staring at the patties when Mom enters the kitchen. I grab the tray and try to slide the batch of baked failure into the trash before she sees it, but the patties hit the bottom of the metal trashcan like stones.

"Dry," Mom says, as she walks past me and over to the freezer. "A little more lard in the dough should fix that."

When her back is to me, I roll my eyes, but I make a mental note to increase the amount of lard in the next batch. I watch Mom examine the freezer. It's been here for two days, and freezer inspection has become a part of her daily routine.

"We *really* can't afford a new freezer," she says, using the hem of her apron to wipe a smudge from the glass.

"We can't afford *not* to have one."

"It *is* nice, though, and it holds more than the old one."

I smile, savoring the small victory.

She's still facing the freezer when she says, "Are you sure you don't want me to come with you tomorrow evening? I can cancel."

Weeks before my invitation to speak at the chamber meeting, Sam surprised Mom with tickets to a play she'd wanted to see for months.

"Mom, we've been over this. I don't want you to cancel. You couldn't have known I'd be invited to speak at the meeting and that the play's final performance would be the same night."

She throws me skeptical look over her shoulder.

"What if I told you your presence would only make me more nervous?"

She smiles. "Like that year we put you in violin and you hid the first few recital flyers?"

I laugh at the memory. "You should be thanking me. I was awful and you know it."

Mom shakes her head and laughs with me, patting my shoulder as she leaves the kitchen. "Yeah, the whole lot of you were awful."

When mom is gone, I check the recipe again, then add more lard to the next batch. When that batch still comes out dry, I add even more, wondering how Dad and Cassie got the original recipe to work. Finally, after two more attempts and just before ten p.m., I extract a perfect batch of patties from the oven.

~

"How did you do it?"

"Who is this?" I ask, even though I recognize Christopher's voice. I tap the speaker button on my cell phone and place it on the edge of the sink.

"You know perfectly well who this is. How did you do it?"

A few minutes before I pulled my perfect batch of patties out of the oven, I got a phone call from Mr. Foster. He'd decided to sign his lease after all. He was pretty sure the Makaos were going to sign theirs too. This call is confirmation they went through with it.

"My assistant says she got a call late this evening. Three additional tenants are signing their leases," he says before I have a chance to speak.

I wipe the condensation from the bathroom mirror and lean in to examine my tired eyes before answering him. "Hello, Christopher. I'm great, thanks," I say, my voice dripping with artificial sweetness. "Did you catch what I just did there? It's something decent people call politeness," I say, emphasizing each syllable of the word *politeness*. "You should try it some time. Not only is it a nice thing to do, sometimes when you're polite, you can persuade people to see things in a whole new light. Maybe help them realize they don't want to throw away everything they've worked so hard for to make some spoiled rich kid even richer."

Christopher grunts. "It's not enough that you're messing with your own future, now you're messing with theirs, too. I hate that you're going to bring them down with you when you fall."

I wipe away the new layer of steam that's formed on the mirror. "Face it, Christopher, you're not as good at playing this game as you thought you were. I have the community's respect and support, I've got the media on my side, and after tomorrow's chamber meeting, I'll have enough new catering customers to pay your ridiculously high rent."

"You sound mighty proud, Free."

"I think I have something to be proud of."

Christopher barks out a laugh. "Bold words for a girl who ran away with her tail tucked between her legs."

"You taught me everything I know about running away."

The line is silent for several beats until he says, "How does that saying go? You know, the one about pride?"

"Look, I was about to get into the shower when you called. If—"

"I remember now," he says, interrupting. "I don't think my mother ever saw the inside of a church, but somehow she always had a proverb handy when it suited her."

"If you're about to quote scripture, you better duck. There's rain in the forecast."

"Chapter sixteen, verse eighteen," he says.

"What?"

"Proverbs."

For a few seconds, all I hear is him breathing and the water running in my shower, then "Good night, Free."

I tap the end button on my phone. I don't have to look up the verse, it's one I know from a childhood spent in Sunday school classes.

Proverbs 16:18—Pride comes before the fall.

CHAPTER SIXTEEN

I lock the front door of the restaurant almost giddy with relief. Today's lunch special was a hit, I've got three baking sheets full of perfectly prepped hors d'oeuvres waiting to be popped into the oven for tonight's chamber meeting, and we've just survived a second visit from Mr. Nelson.

"I have to say," the inspector had said a few minutes earlier, with an expression that suggested he was literally being forced to say it, "I've found no evidence to support the original complaint. I will be closing the file today."

I lean against the counter and take a few minutes to revel in the victory, watching Mr. Nelson leave the restaurant and head out into the rain.

"He's a very uptight young man."

"Mom!" I yell, banging my elbow against the counter as I turn to her. "You have *got* to stop doing that."

"What? It's not like you didn't know I was here." Although she's trying to look innocent, the corner of her mouth is turned up in a smile.

"We passed the inspection," I say, joining her behind

the counter. We stand, side-by-side, chins resting in hands and watch people go by.

"I never doubted for a minute we'd pass, Free. I'm still not pleased you signed that lease, though." She sighs and looks around the restaurant. "There's so much of your father wrapped up in every inch of this place. I know this was his dream for you, but a part of me still wonders if we shouldn't have let it end." Mom pushes herself up from the counter and walks to our booth. I follow, sliding in next to her.

"This was never your dream?"

She fiddles with a condiment holder, sliding it back and forth across the table. "When I was only a few years younger than you are now, the only thing I wanted was to be happy. Does that sound selfish?"

I shake my head, although I can't reconcile the stories I'd heard from Mom about her volunteering for organizations that sent her to the Caribbean and Africa, with the woman sitting across from me telling me that happiness was her only goal.

"Happy looks like different things to different people, Free. I didn't know what my happy would be, but I thought it would always involve me traveling and doing service around the world."

"Then meeting Dad changed all that," I say.

Mom takes a deep breath. "Your father seemed to have been born knowing what made him happy. Cooking was it for him."

"So, you joined him here in Pointe Hill, and that changed everything for you."

"Yes."

"And so did having me." I look outside. The rain is

coming down heavier and the sidewalk traffic has thinned. Mom touches my arm, and I look at her.

"You know how you came by the name Freedom, don't you?"

A smile tugs at the corner of my mouth. "The name Freedom," my mom is known for saying to anyone who asks, and many who do not, "is my homage to a time in my life when I fought for freedom for those who could not." From apartheid in South Africa to childhood hunger in America, Agnes Webb spent most of her premarital years crisscrossing the globe as an activist.

"Yes, I know," I answer, widening my smile, even as I remember all the times I came home crying after being teased about my name, wishing I had a *normal* name like Mary or Becky.

We sit for a few minutes, contemplating what we've just shared, until Mom asks, "You sure you don't mind about tonight?"

"Mom," I begin, chuckling. "This is like the tenth time you've asked. I promise I'm okay with it."

She reaches around her neck and tugs gently at the ring on her necklace, pulling it from side to side, making a soft zipping sound with it.

"Do you *want* to go out tonight?" I ask, as the realization hits me that my mom might be as nervous about her date as I am about my meeting.

She looks up then answers my question with one of her own. "Do you think it's too soon? With Sam, I mean."

There's an awkward silence as we both try to register the fact that my mom has just asked me for dating advice. I don't know what she wants to hear, what answer will make her feel like it's okay, because a part of me still feels as though without dad, our lives will never really be okay again. But I tell the truth, even though it hurts to admit it.

"Daddy was sick for a long time, Mom. I didn't realize how sick until I came back home to help." I take her hand and snake my fingers through hers. "This is the most excited I've seen you in a long time. I still miss Dad a lot, and I know you miss him, too. But he would want you to be happy."

Mom blows out a long, shaky breath and squeezes my hand, then we both turn and watch through the window as the rain falls.

THE RAIN IS BEATING HARD AGAINST THE ROOF WHEN I put the hors d'oeuvres into the oven and set the timer. I pack the condiments and utensils in a bag for later, and I'm carrying a large tray to the sink when my phone rings. I grab it, holding the phone between my ear and shoulder. "Hello?"

"Free," Iris says.

This is the first time she's called me today. If things had been okay between us, Iris and I would have been on the phone all day, me telling her how nervous I am and she saying any and everything to help calm my nerves. I miss her, and I'm so glad to hear from her, I stop packing supplies and an apology starts tumbling from my lips. "Iris, I'm *so* sorry. I know you were just trying to protect me and to keep the promise you made to—"

"Go to the *Post*'s home page," Iris blurts out.

"Are you still mad at me?"

"Just go to the website, Free. Please."

"What am I looking for?" I ask as I wipe my hands on my apron and head to the office to grab my laptop.

There's a pause on the line, then she says, "You'll know when you see it."

I click on my bookmark tab, strumming my fingers while the picture on the front page of the *Pointe Hill Post* reveals itself slowly. Pixel-by-pixel, the image appears until it's clear that it's a picture of me taken the night of the CHI event. In the picture, I'm holding a plate with a huge slice of chocolate cake on it. The heading above the article reads: "Local Restaurant Owner Wants Her Cake and Wants to Eat It Too."

I laugh nervously, "The title's not so bad. Makes me sound kind of sassy."

"Keep reading," Iris says softly.

I swallow hard. "How bad can it be?"

"It's not just about the restaurant, Free."

I read the byline—Vanessa Marlow—and though I know I've heard that name before, I can't immediately place it. My eyes drop to the beginning of the article, and the first paragraph stops me cold.

"Freedom Spalding, daughter of the late Raymond Spalding and his wife Agnes, might seem like she's just what this community needs in its fight for a seat at the development table, but a recent investigation into Ms. Spalding's past reveals she's not what she appears to be."

"Investigation? Why would the *Post* be investigating me?" I ask, choking out the words. I sit on the edge of the couch, my fingers trembling as I scroll down the page.

"Following her father's death, Ms. Spalding emerged as a voice for long-time residents who felt excluded from the area's drive for growth and expansion. Last month Ms. Spalding made an impassioned plea for developer Chronus

Holdings Incorporated (CHI) to adopt a more inclusive real estate development plan. Her speech had community members and anti-gentrification advocates alike believing they'd found a champion in Freedom Spalding.

"Yet the Post has discovered another side of the restaurateur turned local hero. The Post has obtained records that reveal that prior to returning to Pointe Hill, Ms. Spalding was employed with Berry & Barlow, a corporation currently under investigation for predatory lending practices that target low-income and minority homebuyers. Ms. Spalding worked for Berry & Barlow for two years, and former colleagues reported that she rose quickly through company ranks, being promoted from a junior marketing associate to a senior marketing manager in under two years.

Ms. Spalding's departure from the company, just days before the government investigation was made public, raises several questions. How much did Ms. Spalding know about the company's illegal practices? Did she participate in any of these practices? And why, just days before returning to Pointe Hill, was Ms. Spalding fired from the company?"

"Free?" Iris's voice breaks through my mental fog.

"Yeah." My voice sounds thin and fragile, even to my own ears.

"Did you know about the predatory lending?"

"Not when I started working there. I swear. And when I found out, I tried to document everything I found." I scan the rest of the article as fast as I can, my heart thumping against my chest. All the while Iris peppers me with questions.

"How long did you know? What did you try to do about it?"

I scan the page quickly, ignoring Iris's questions. *Please don't let it be here.* I can't read the article fast enough. I don't want anyone here to know. I left that all behind me for a reason. I stop scrolling halfway down the screen. The headache starts then, the first tentacle tapping a rhythm against my left temple.

"Free? They're saying . . ." Iris begins, but I barely hear her because I've found it. I read to myself at the same time Iris reads it aloud.

"According to former colleagues, the then twenty-three-year-old manager was terminated after it was uncovered that she was having an affair with a married Berry & Barlow senior executive."

CHAPTER SEVENTEEN

"Free?" Iris's pleads from the other end of the line.

"I swear I didn't know he was married, Iris. No one in the office did. He lied to me."

Thoughts swirl around my head like a word-cloud. The meeting tonight. What will they all think when they learn I worked for a company that victimized the kinds of communities I claim I want to serve? And Mom, Oh God, Mom. I can't even imagine what she's going to think when she reads it.

A wave of nausea hits me as the ache in my head sharpens. I slide the laptop onto the floor and lie back on the couch.

"Free? You still there?"

"I thought I'd left all of that behind me," I say, the tears at the back of my throat muffling my words. "My past just won't leave me alone."

There's a pause on the line, then Iris says, "I'm supposed to be headed into a meeting with Simone. Let me tell her I've got a family emergency then I'll be right over."

"The chamber meeting is tonight," I say, groaning. "I can't face them, Iris."

"Go to the meeting and finish what you started. I'll come over as soon as I can."

I nod, even though I'm aware Iris can't see it through the phone. I close my eyes and cover my ears with my hands, hoping to quiet the pounding in my head. But the pounding grows more intense each time I rehash the blog post in my head.

Then suddenly I remember where I'd seen the name from the article's byline. She was a reporter at the CHI event, the groupie who was clinging to Christopher most of the night. Was Christopher behind this? And if he was, how did he find out about the relationship? Interoffice romances were against company policy, so we'd been discrete.

The questions whirl around inside my head until the pounding becomes so intense, my eyes feel like they're vibrating. I grab two migraine pills from my desk drawer, swallow them, then return to the couch, praying for some relief from the pounding. And just when I think I can't take any more, I drift into a deep, merciful sleep.

THE BEEPING IS CONSTANT. AT FIRST I THINK IT'S coming from the monitors in my dad's hospital room, but the sound keeps getting louder, and the louder it gets the more intense the smell that accompanies it.

Then suddenly, I realize the beeping isn't coming from my dad's hospital bed. It's the oven timer. And the smell is an oven full of burned hors d'oeuvres.

I'm instantly awake and jump off the couch and dash

into the kitchen. When I open the oven door, smoke wafts out, sending me into a coughing fit. I turn the oven off and begin removing the trays of burned pastries.

The throbbing in my head returns and brings with it a reminder of what sent me on my crying jag in the first place: my past neatly summarized in a five-hundred-word blog post.

By now I'm sure most of Pointe Hill have read it, including Mom. I check my phone and my call history is lit up with missed calls and texts. A few from Iris and Anthony, a handful from other friends, one voicemail from my mother. And one missed call from Christopher. *Pride comes before the fall*, he'd said last night. I never imagined he would orchestrate a fall this big.

I wash my face in the bathroom sink and when I return to the kitchen, the rows of blackened pastries lined up on the baking sheets stare up at me like mutinous soldiers.

"I'd rebel too, if I were you," I say. Offering them a mock salute, I slump onto a stool and look up at my grandmother's picture.

"Oh, Grandma, what would you do?"

"She'd grab the dough from the refrigerator and start peeling plantains."

I spin around on the stool.

Mom, decked out in a sleek red dress, hose, and heels, stands in the doorway. "And she wouldn't waste time talking to the food."

"What are you doing here?"

"I figured you could use a hand tonight."

I search her face for any sign of disappointment, any indication she's read the article. I see none, but somehow I know she's read it.

My fear of disappointing her starts the flow of tears I

thought I'd finished shedding for the night. "Mom, the minute I realized what was happening at the company, I went to my boss. He told me I'd gotten it all wrong. That they were actually helping people get homes who wouldn't have been able to afford them otherwise. They said a competitor was spreading false rumors about them. I believed him. About that and everything else. I was so stupid."

Mom rushes over and wraps her arms around me. "Shh, it will be okay, honey."

I sniffle, my tears staining her beautiful red dress, but she just holds me tighter and strokes my hair. When the tears stop falling and I take a deep breath, Mom gives me one last squeeze, then steps back and examines the charred scene on the counter.

"How you let the food burn so, Free?"

Although my head still hurts and my eyes are stinging, I laugh at the matter-of-fact way Mom says this, as though burning the trays of food was all part of my master plan.

"I fell asleep," I say, shrugging and flicking one of the hors d'oeuvres. "Not like I'm going to need them anyway."

Mom stops picking at the carnage on the tray and whips her head around. "Why wouldn't you need hors d oeuvres for tonight?"

I look at her incredulously. "I can't go tonight. At best they think I'm some simple girl who got taken advantage of by a corporate executive. At worst, they think I'm a hypocrite who lied about having their best interests at heart. I can't face those people, Mom."

"Freedom Isabelle Spalding," she says, hands perched on her hips, "I raised you better than that. You are going to go to that meeting tonight and show those people you are cut from Spalding stock. From your grandmother and grandfather down to your father and me. We don't give up that easy."

When I just blink at her without answering, she raises an eyebrow.

"Yes, ma'am," I say, managing another smile.

She eyes the burned trays and says, "So, we'll make some plantain tarts. Yours are as good as your dad's."

The mention of my dad threatens another wave of tears, but I swallow them as I watch Mom take off her bangles and her watch, and tie her apron around her waist.

"Those plantains aren't going to peel themselves," she says, tilting her head toward the pantry.

I head to the pantry, but stop halfway there. "Won't Sam be disappointed about you canceling tonight?"

She waves me off. "He's fine." The corners of her mouth hitch into a smile before she adds, "He said there'd be lots of other plays and lots of other nights. As many and as often as I wanted them." Then Mom does something I don't think I've ever seen her do—she blushes.

"You're blushing," I say, laughing.

She swats a dishtowel in my direction. "Stop being so fast, girl."

I bring an armful of plantains to the counter and stand next to her. "I'm still sorry I ruined your night."

"I would never consider a night spent with my girl ruined."

I lean over and tap my shoulder against hers.

"Now hurry up. Those plantains are not going to peel themselves."

"Yes, ma'am," I say, and offer a salute before I pick up the knife and begin peeling.

CHAPTER EIGHTEEN

The sky opens up as Mom and I run from the truck to the meeting space, and we're soaked by the time we get to the door. We're running late, and I can see through the glass in the door that the meeting has already started. Around fifty people are in attendance, and I recognize many of my neighbors and long-time restaurant patrons. The Fosters are seated near the front. Mr. Makao and his mother are there, too. Next to them are Simon Thibodeaux and his daughters Nia and Rachel. The Thibdodeauxs own a large medical supply distribution company here in Pointe Hill. They are powerful allies, and the smiles on their faces let me know that at least I have them in my corner.

Mr. Wilcox, one of our local representatives, is behind the podium addressing the audience. Mom and I exchange glances then I open the door as quietly as possible. But the door creaks, alerting everyone to our arrival. Mr. Wilcox pauses as the attendees turn to stare. Mrs. Kimble, the neighborhood gossip, glares at me. I paint on a smile and offer a feeble wave. A few people wave back.

Mom and I are quietly laying the food out on a table in the back of the room when I feel a tap on my shoulder.

"You made it," Sandra Kane says.

I clear my throat before answering. "I've been looking forward to this night for weeks."

"Well, yes, but you were late, and I thought maybe . . ."

She trails off, but she doesn't need to finish for me to know what she's thinking. I look away, my skin hot with embarrassment.

"Sandra," Mom says, sidling up beside me and extending her hand. "I know I haven't been to a meeting since before Raymond got sick, but I'm sure you understand what a hectic time it's been for us."

Sandra shakes her head, "Yes, we miss you and Raymond too, of course. He was an asset to the chamber. He's been sorely missed."

"That's why I appreciate you giving Free the opportunity to address the group tonight. It would have meant a lot to her father."

Sandra, who's been nodding the entire time Mom has been speaking, glances at the audience, then gestures for us to move in closer.

"Look, Free, personally I don't care what happened before you came back home. I believe you when you say you care about the community, and I've seen what you've done at your parents' place. That goes a long way with me, but you know most of the folks here tonight. Many of them have already been burned by people coming here and promising to do good."

"But, I'm not just *people*, Sandra. My dad was their colleague, my mom still is. What I did before I came back here shouldn't define who I am now."

"I understand that, but you can appreciate that there are a few people here tonight who might not feel the same."

"Sandra," I begin, and someone in the back row looks in our direction. I hunch closer to her and lower my voice. "I know no matter what I say there are a few people who will have already made up their minds, but I don't want to run away from this."

She sighs. "You're Raymond's kid, alright." She looks up at the clock on the wall behind us. "You're scheduled to speak last and you'll have about fifteen minutes. Good luck, Free. I think you'll need it."

THE ROOM IS BUZZING AS I WALK UP TO THE PODIUM, but you could hear a pin drop by the time I stand behind it. I look out at the audience. Many of them wear neutral expressions, a few are friendly, but some look downright angry. Mrs. Kimble is scowling.

I tap the mike and lean in. "Thank you," I begin, but my voice cracks and the microphone squeals, eliciting a few muffled groans from the audience. I step back, suddenly overwhelmed by the heat from the lights in the room.

I take a deep breath, then close my eyes for a second to try to regroup. The door squeaks and when I open my eyes, Iris and Anthony are standing at the back of the room next to my mother. Their presence provides the reinforcement I need to find my voice.

"Good evening. My name is Freedom Spalding, and my mother and I own Cecelia's restaurant in the Old Sixth Ward. I appreciate the opportunity to address you this evening, and I want to especially thank the Fosters and the Makaos for entrusting me with leading this committee.

"Before I begin sharing my thoughts on how I believe we can flourish in this changing landscape, I'd like to address the elephant in the room." I pause to take a sip of water from the glass on the podium and steel my reserve. "I know most of you have read the blog post that came out today. I wish I could tell you that everything in that article is a lie, but I can't. What I can do is clarify a few things. First, I was fired from Berry & Barlow, but not because of a relationship with an executive. I was fired for emails I sent to the executive committee questioning the company's marketing practices."

Mrs. Kimble's husband raises his hand, but starts speaking before I acknowledge him. "So you *did* know what the company was doing, but you stayed anyway. The only conclusion I can come to is that you stayed because you were paid well and you thought maybe if you kept quiet, you'd keep getting paid." In the audience, murmurs of agreement rise.

"We know you care about your dad's restaurant," he continues, "but if you're only back here because you ran out of other options, what happens when something better comes along? How do we know that at the first good paying offer, you won't just pick up and leave and end up working for the other side again?"

"Yeah," an older gentleman I recognize as one of the deacons from my mom's church, pipes up from the back row. "I read about Berry & Barlow in the papers. They baited homeowners into getting mortgages they couldn't afford. Hundreds of them lost their homes. And now we learn you were a part of all of it."

"I worked in the marketing department," I interrupt,

but my explanation is barely heard as Mr. Kimble cuts in again.

"Why should we trust you to lead this committee? Why should we trust you at all?"

Heads are nodding throughout the audience, and I have to raise my voice to be heard. "You should trust me because I *do* believe in this community and all of you. I was twenty-one years old and fresh out of college when I started at Berry & Barlow; I was excited about the prospect of working my way up through a company that helped people. But that changed when I realized what they were all about. I admit I was uncertain about my future when I returned to Pointe Hill. But it's been a year, and I'm still here. And I've stayed because I believe in my father's dream. I believe the Pointe Hill I grew up in is worth preserving, and I believe all of us in this room have the power to do it."

"How long did you know about what they were doing?" a woman calls out. "Why didn't you leave sooner?" comes another voice from the crowd. Someone else asks when I first learned about the company's illegal practices. Another wants to know if I was paid to keep silent. The questions keep coming faster than I can process them and, overwhelmed, I step back from the mike.

Mr. Foster stands and pumps his hands to silence the audience. When it's quiet, he says, "I think we should give the young lady a chance. She understands business. She's shared her ideas with my wife and me, and I believe her ideas can help all of us run our businesses better."

"So we're okay with her taking on a leadership role on this committee? We have an awful lot riding here. Do we want to place that on someone we don't even know we can trust?" the deacon asks.

"We all know Agnes, and we all knew Raymond." He

points to me. "She is their daughter, and any child of Raymond's is one I know I can trust."

"Her father would be ashamed of her," Mrs. Kimble spits out. Immediately the crowd grows quiet.

I glance up, looking for my mother at the back of the room, and I see her poised and ready to march up the center aisle and give Mrs. Kimble a piece of her mind. But I hold up my hand to stop her. This is my battle, and I have to fight it without her.

"Free," Mrs. Kimble continues, "we are all aware of your father's contributions to this community, and we are grateful for them. " She turns to face the room. "But let's not forget about Ms. Spalding's," she purses her lips as though she's just sucked on a lemon, "indiscretion. That speaks to her character, and I don't know about you, but I think anyone who can so easily do something like that can't be trusted with anything." She lowers her head and moves closer to her husband then peers at the audience over the rim of her glasses, "or with anyone."

Mrs. Kimble's words zip through me like an electric shock. I want to scream that I didn't know. That I'd never knowingly enter a relationship with a married man. But I also want to wag my finger in her face and deliver a sermon about judgment. As I step back from the mike, my mind races to come up with the best way to handle the situation.

"Ms. Spalding's personal life should have no bearing whatsoever on the subject at hand. If none of us were allowed to support ideas we believe in because of things we've done in the past, not one of us would be in this room tonight."

The statement and the person delivering it send another jolt of electricity through me. Christopher is standing at the back of the room. He unbuttons his suit jacket and walks up the middle aisle, stopping when he reaches the podium. His jaw is clenched, his face stern, but when our eyes meet, I see that his are soft, the edges marked with hurt.

He turns to face the audience. "Ms. Spalding and I may not see eye-to-eye on this issue, but it benefits no one to pull private matters onto a public stage. I ask that you all afford her the benefit of judging her *ideas*, instead of her." He turns to me. "Ms. Spalding."

Christopher walks down the aisle, nods at my mother, then takes a seat in the back row. The shock of seeing him here, and then having him defend me, is almost too much to handle. But I manage to pull myself together and address the audience once again.

"I'm not asking you to trust me blindly. I'm just asking that you hear me out. Listen to my ideas and give me a chance to show you what I can do. If I fail, if my ideas don't work, or if I give you any reason to question my loyalty," I turn to Mrs. Kimble, "or my integrity, I'll gladly step aside."

More heads are nodding now than were a few minutes ago. I reiterate the sentiments I first expressed at the CHI event. Some of the wariness I'd seen earlier in the audience has morphed into hopefulness, but I still have my work cut out for me.

Christopher stands as I'm wrapping up, and by the time Sandra returns to the podium to dismiss the group, he's left the room.

"You did good, Free. Really good," Mom says.

"Thanks for everything tonight," I say, hugging her. "Anthony, did you skip class because of me?"

He winks. "Was totally worth it. No worries, Danielle's taking notes for me."

I hug Iris. "Don't get all mushy on me," she says, but she hugs me tightly and keeps hugging me for a long time. When we release each other, she says, "What was up with Christopher?"

"Girl, I have no idea. I didn't even know he'd be here."

"Do you think he was behind the blog post?"

"I did, but now . . ."

"Well, I wouldn't go awarding him any honor badges just yet. That speech he gave could have been guilt talking."

Iris and I don't have time to finish our conversation as people begin making their way to the hors d'oeuvres.

Everything we made is a hit, and near the end of the evening when we're packing up, one of the women from the audience approaches me. "Ms. Spalding, Carmen Holmes," she says, shaking my hand. When she releases my hand I hold it behind my back and flex my fingers to get the blood flowing again. I thought my mom's handshake was numbing. "That was impressive," she continues.

"Thank you. My dad's recipes." I pull Mom closer. "And my mom's hard work."

"The food was excellent, but I was also referring to your talk." Carmen gently tugs at the starched white collar of her dress shirt then looks over my shoulder and angles her head toward an empty room behind us. "Can we talk for a few minutes?"

In the privacy of the room, Carmen reveals her reason for wanting to speak to me. "I work for a national organization that provides seed money for companies that are revitalizing low- and middle-income communities for the people who live there." She takes a business card from her pocket. "With your background in marketing and the insights you gained while working for Berry & Barlow, I think you could do amazing things on a national level."

"But Pointe Hill needs my help, too," I say.

"And you'll still be able to help, you just would be doing so on a broader scale and from our corporate office in DC." She presses her business card into my hand. "I know this is a lot to absorb. But in this position, you could help thousands, compared to the dozens you'd be helping if you stay in Pointe Hill. And it pays well enough that you'd be able to continue supporting your mom financially. Just think about it. I don't need an answer today." She takes my hand, gives it another brisk pump then walks out of the room.

Back in the main room Mom is packing up the leftovers. She looks up when I approach. "What was that about?"

I shrug. "Nothing to worry about. Why don't you head home, and I'll clean up here and get a ride home with Iris."

"If you're sure," she says, too tired to put up a fight.

"Yeah, I'll be fine." I kiss her cheek and wave goodbye as she heads out.

The room empties and when Iris and I are alone, I say, "The reporter who wrote the blog post was Christopher's groupie from the CHI event."

She clucks her tongue. "You know I have my Taser in my purse."

"I'm not even going to ask why you're telling me about the Taser in your purse," I say, chuckling.

"You know where he lives, and we want answers, right? I'm just saying, a little jolt of electricity never hurt anybody."

"Hurting people is *exactly* what jolts of electricity do."

"I *said* a little."

"No Taser. I'm going to have to find another way to deal with Christopher. But not now. I don't think I can handle anymore drama tonight."

CHAPTER NINETEEN

"I knew he'd changed, but I never imagined he'd dig up dirt on me and have one of his groupies publish it," I say, pulling my T-shirt over my head and tossing it into the hamper.

Iris is lying on her stomach, stretched out across my bed. "That was low, even for a Bellamy."

She pauses, and I stop rummaging through my dresser and look at her.

"Why didn't you tell me about Bryan or all the stuff going on with Berry & Barlow before tonight?"

I'd told Iris the whole story in the car on the way here, including all the sordid details about my relationship with Bryan, the Berry & Barlow executive. I put on a clean T-shirt and join her on the bed. "You and I didn't talk much anymore. I can't tell you the number of times I thought about calling you, telling you everything that was going on, but I was ashamed. Ashamed I'd let our friendship get to the point where I couldn't just pick up the phone and call you. Ashamed about the mess I'd gotten myself into with

Bryan." I run my hand across the back of my neck. "What is it with me and unavailable men, Iris?"

She rolls onto her back. "It's not just you. We want to fix them. Save them from themselves. But who's going to save us?"

We're quiet for some time until I say, "I'm so sorry we argued. I was hurt because you'd kept what you knew about Christopher from me and because this was something else you and mom shared that I wasn't a part of."

"You had every right to be hurt. I should have told you. And if I'm being honest, I was hurt, too. I was hurt because you ended up with Jason that night."

I open my mouth to object, but Iris raises a hand to stop me. "I know nothing happened between the two of you, but a part of me was hurt you turned to him instead of me."

"You were in New York," I remind her.

"But I would have been on the first plane out if you'd told me to come. After you called, you hung up on me and stopped taking my calls."

"I didn't plan to go off with Jason that night. They were retiring his football jersey and he was at the school to receive a plaque during a special ceremony they were having for him. I was a mess after I saw Christopher and Jessica together. When I got off the phone with you, I ran outside and Jason ran after me.

"We jumped in his car and he drove around for a while. He was using a crutch because of his knee, and when the pain got too bad, he stopped and bought some alcohol. We went back to Cecelia's and spent the rest of the night drinking and talking."

I tell Iris everything I told Jason that night. How humiliated I'd felt when I saw Christopher walking into the gym with Jessica. How it was Jessica's hair that caught my eye first. Pinned-up perfection, the disco ball hanging from the ceiling reflecting prisms of light off her auburn hair. And I tell her everything Jason shared with me about how afraid he'd been on the night of the accident when he thought his mother wouldn't make it. How he thought his life would be nothing if he couldn't play football, and why he felt such guilt over the accident.

"I think what hurt the most about you not telling me about Christopher is that you were probably right not to. Because despite everything he did, I would have taken him back." I pause and take a deep breath to steady my voice, but it doesn't work. The words tumble from my mouth, shaky and jagged as if saying them rattles my very core. "I still believed he loved me, and because I believed that, I couldn't stop loving him. Not that night or the morning after. Not that entire summer before I went away to college. Believe me, I tried. But loving someone shouldn't be that hard."

"Do you still believe he really loved you?"

"Believe?" I bark out a harsh laugh. "What I believe doesn't matter. Now I go by what I see. And what I see is a man who doesn't care who he hurts as long as he gets what he wants."

"For what it's worth, I didn't think you were weak for wanting him back." Iris leans into me until her shoulder presses against mine. "You know all those trips up to New York? They weren't just about seeing my friends. It was about Manuel."

Manuel is Iris's on-again, off-again boyfriend. Back when we were teenagers, their relationship was the stuff of high school legend. At one point they were even talking marriage, but since their last breakup, Iris doesn't talk about him much, and I know enough not to ask.

"I don't know if we ever get over our first love," Iris says.

"If the way I'm feeling about Christopher tonight is any indication, we get over them."

We both laugh then lie quietly, staring up at the ceiling fan. A few minutes later Iris's phone buzzes. She grabs it out of her purse and knits her brow as she scans the screen.

"Who's that?" I ask, propping myself up on my elbows.

"A work thing. I've still got a presentation to prepare tonight. I should head home . . . unless you want me to stay."

"Nah, go ahead. I'm gonna binge-watch *How To Get Away with Murder* on Netflix."

"Take notes," she says, hopping off the bed and pulling me into a hug. "We might need those skills tomorrow. Along with this." She pats her purse, alluding to the Taser.

"Iris," I say, my voice a warning.

She raises her hands and backs away, laughing. "I'm just saying . . ."

I walk her out then head to the kitchen. I'm rummaging through the refrigerator when the rain, which had eased up while we were at the meeting, announces its return with a flash of lightning and a crack of thunder. The lightning illuminates Iris's forgotten umbrella on my living room floor. I'm wishing I'd asked her to stay, when the doorbell rings.

I run to the front door and pull it open. "I was just—" Even with the blown light bulb above my stoop, I can clearly make out the outline of Christopher's face.

When he steps forward, his eyes are slits against the pelting rain. *Good for the rain*, I think, *pounding on him the way I want to*. I can hear him breathing hard, even over the sound of the rain pinging against the metal awning above my door. "What are you doing here?"

"I came to talk. There are things we need to get out in the open."

"Like telling me what you had to do with that blog post?"

Christopher doesn't answer.

I shake my head. "Every time I think you can't dig any deeper you throw more dirt over your shoulder." I step back and push the door to close it, but Christopher stops it with his hand.

"I deserve that," he says, blinking the rain out of his eyes.

"You deserve a hell of a lot more than that."

"I didn't know the article would say those things. When Vanessa asked for an interview, she said she wanted to talk about my plans for phase two of CHI's development project."

"How did she find out where I worked? And how did she find out about Bryan?"

"Was that his name? It wasn't in the article," he says, before realizing that was probably the wrong question to ask me.

I push the door, but he stops it again. "Can I come in?" he asks, hunching his shoulders against the rain. "Please, just give me five minutes."

Thunder cracks in the distance, surprising me. I jump and Christopher reaches out to steady me, keeping his hand on my arm longer than he needs to. When he lowers his hand, I step out of the way and motion for him to enter, closing the door behind me and walking into my living room. "You have five minutes."

Christopher doesn't say anything as drops of water from his soaked clothes fall onto my carpet. He stands in the middle of my living room, pinching his nose and shaking his head, spraying water across the floor.

I sigh, then walk to the bathroom to grab a towel, stopping to look at myself in the mirror. I pull the scrunchie from my hair, comb my fingers through my braids, and take a few deep breaths before heading out of the bathroom. Halfway to the living room I remember why I went into the bathroom in the first place. "Get it together, Spalding," I mumble as I double back and grab a towel from the linen closet.

When I return to the living room, Christopher is looking at my college graduation picture on the wall. I clear my throat and he turns, a little red cheeked, maybe from the rain or maybe from being caught studying my photo. I can't tell.

"Your hair was different," he says, angling his head toward the picture.

"I wore it straight back then." When I started at Brandton, I was determined to be someone other than who I'd been in Pointe Hill. The transformation included biweekly hair straightening sessions at a salon.

"You looked good." He turns and flits his eyes over me. "*Look* good."

"You're down to four minutes," I say, determined not to be taken in by Christopher's intense gaze. I toss the towel at him then sit on the couch. He rubs the towel roughly across his hair before he lets it fall around his neck as he looks around my apartment.

"Three minutes."

"I don't know where she got that information about you or why she published it," he says hastily.

"How could you *not know*? You certainly didn't look

like a couple with secrets the night I saw the two of you together."

"We're not a couple," he corrects. "Do you really think I'd do something like that to you? I wouldn't drag your dirty laundry out to win a fight. I've got way too much dirty laundry of my own to try to use it against someone I . . ." he trails off without completing the thought.

"So, why did she do it, Christopher? And how did she find out about Bryan?"

"I don't know, Free, but I *will* find out. I promise you."

"Your promises don't hold much water with me."

"I know, but this time I'm in control of what happens or doesn't happen with us, and I'm telling you, I'll fix this."

"It's late, and I don't want to do this now." I close my eyes and bend my head from side to side, stretching out the tightness in my neck. I feel the couch depress next to me and Christopher's damp shirt brushes against my arm. Half of me wants to lean into him, the other half wants to flee.

"I saw you, you know," he says quietly. "That day you came to my office, I saw you from my window. I spend a lot of time looking through those windows. You stopped in front of the building and looked up. Even from that distance I knew it was you. I knew you couldn't see me, but—"

"Why are you telling me this?" I ask, my eyes still closed. When he doesn't answer, I look at him.

"Because I want you to know I had an unfair advantage that day. I had time to prepare myself. Time to make sure I didn't react when you walked through the door. Time to pretend that seeing you didn't affect me." His gaze skips across my face, lingers on my lips. "I don't know if any amount of time would have been enough, though. "

"Christopher . . ."

"I didn't come here tonight thinking we could just bury

the hatchet. But maybe we can move forward. I meant what I said at the meeting. We don't have to be our pasts. Your ideas deserve to be heard. If we can't be friends, maybe we can at least not be enemies."

I look at his damp hair and shirt, his pants, still wet from the rain. This isn't the same man who shot dagger-shaped words through my heart weeks ago. It isn't the man who taunted me with a Bible verse two days ago. But this isn't Christopher, either. Not my Christopher. Still, if there's even a possibility he'll listen to my ideas about the community, a temporary truce with him might be a means to an end.

I lean back on the sofa. "Well, I do have a few ideas I'd like to run by you. I know it's not what you may have had in mind for your project, but it's a good plan, and if you would just look at it, I think you'd agree."

"I'd love to take a look," Christopher says.

"Now?"

"Why not? Unless you have somewhere else to be."

"No," I answer, quickly. "I'll grab my notes."

As I walk past him, my leg brushes against his and he takes my hand, wrapping his fingers around it. I look down at his hand clasped around mine.

"Free?"

I don't want to look into his eyes. I'm not ready for what I think I'll see in them.

"Look at me, please."

My gaze travels slowly, up from our joined hands, over the shirt clinging to his chest, then linger on his Adam's apple rising and falling as he swallows. Finally, I look into his eyes.

"I'm sorry," he whispers, scanning my face as he squeezes my fingers. "For everything."

His voice is soft, somber. I drag my gaze away from his and study our hands. Despite everything that has passed between us, it still feels so natural to have my hand in his. But when he moves to squeeze my fingers again, I pull from his grip. "I'll be right back with the notes."

I walk to my room, close the door behind me, and let out a long breath. As I gather the papers, I remind myself that I've only invited Christopher into my apartment, not into my life. "This is no big deal," I say to myself. Then again, "This is no big deal." So, why does it feel like the biggest deal I've made in a really long time?

CHAPTER TWENTY

Christopher has been reviewing my notes for over an hour, and I've been sipping from a bottle of ginger beer and stealing glances at him the entire time, pretending I'm not a little freaked out he's here.

I gave him one of my oversized Brandton University sweatshirts to wear so he wouldn't have to sit around in a wet shirt. And so I wouldn't have to *see* him sitting around in a wet shirt. Even though it's snug on him and smells like lavender fabric softener, he's unquestionably masculine and undeniably distracting. When he leans in, pointing at one of the papers in his hand, the press of his thigh against mine tests my resolve.

"So what you're proposing is a partnership between Pointe Hill State's mentoring program and these merchants," he says, tapping the paperwork.

"Yes," I say quickly, shifting so his thigh no longer touches mine. "These students are talented. They're future graphic designers, programmers, ad execs. I want to tap their skills to help the businesses in the Old Sixth."

"How does CHI fit in?"

I scoot forward on the couch and flip through the papers, stopping when I get to the page that lists the resources the program needs to get off the ground. "They'll need funding for computers and software, and they need mentors and volunteers. "

Christopher studies the figures while I watch nervously. "And what would CHI receive in return?"

"If these businesses make money CHI will, too. You'll get your rent increase, maybe not right away, but when they start doing better they'll be able to pay higher rents. And you can't put a dollar amount on the PR you'll get by working with the merchants in the Old Sixth Ward instead of against them. We just need a few months to establish the program and begin pairing students with merchants."

Christopher grabs his bottle from my coffee table and leans back on the couch. "I can tell you now, this is going to be a tough sell with Jason. But let me look at these numbers some more and put a meeting together for us to discuss this with him." He takes a swig from the bottle then holds it up and examines it. "I haven't had a ginger beer in years. Remember how we used to guzzle them like water?"

"I still do," I answer, smiling at the memory of sneaking bottles out of the cooler and drinking them on the steps behind the restaurant. "Mom would have killed me if she'd known how much of the inventory I drank." But the memory is tempered with sadness.

While he stares at the bottle in his hand, I stare at him. "Why did you do it?" I ask, looking away and using my fingernail to pick at the damp label on my bottle.

"I told you, I didn't tell Vanessa anything about—"

"Not the article. Jessica."

I wait for his answer but remind myself that I was the one who said I didn't want to walk through the ruins.

Christopher scrubs a hand across the back of his neck, then says, "It's . . . complicated."

"Complicated how?"

"I never wanted anyone to get hurt."

"That's not an answer. Complicated *how*?"

"There was just a lot going on," he says.

The exasperated tone in his voice pisses me off. I pick up my drink, then snatch his from his hand. "Not good enough." His answer satisfies nothing, fixes nothing. Changes nothing. I was a fool to ask and a fool to think any answer he'd give would bring me some kind of closure. I take the bottles to the kitchen.

"Wait, Free, it's . . ." but I don't hear the rest. I'm already throwing the bottles in the recyclables container when he enters the kitchen.

"My father had these expectations—"

I slam the lid back on the recycling can. "Oh come on, you can do better than that. Your dad *made* you take Jessica to the prom? He *made* you break two years of promises to me?"

"I was an eighteen-year-old kid."

"And I was seventeen! Seventeen and in love and foolishly making plans for a future with someone who had no intention of being a part of it."

"That's not fair," he says, moving closer. "I admit I made mistakes, but you'd think with everything you've done—"

"You have some nerve!" I yell, pinning him with my gaze. "I knew what you said at the meeting was too good to be true. I guess the only past you want people to forgive is your own."

Christopher stabs a finger in my direction. "No, *you're* the one with the nerve. You're sitting here judging me for mistakes I made as a kid, when you've obviously made some pretty big—" He stops himself, but it's too late.

"Get out!"

He doesn't move an inch. "I'm not going anywhere until we finish this. Obviously we've both been holding on to a bunch of shit for seven years. Let's just finish it."

"Oh, believe me, it's finished."

"I wanted to take you to the prom," he blurts out. "It was the *only* thing I wanted to do. I'd looked forward to it from the day I first met you. And when I was at that prep school senior year with those girls who couldn't have cared less about anything but who my dad was and what going out with me could do for them, all I could think about was that you wouldn't have cared about any of that. I wanted to call you, wanted to hear your voice, but I thought staying away from you was for the best."

"Best for you!" I yell.

"No, not being able to see you, to talk to you, it killed me inside!"

I take a deep breath to try to steady my shaking voice. "I called, texted, wrote you emails every day that summer before senior year. You never answered."

Christopher groans. "I did answer."

"A few emails when you first got to Europe. That was it. I deserved better than that."

"You did, and I'm so sorry, Free. I know how much that must have hurt you, but by that time everything was out of control. My father was a manipulative son of a bitch. Once he came back into our lives, he controlled every aspect of it, including who Jason and I could and could not see." He moves closer. "Please try to understand. When he took us to Europe that summer he made it clear that if we didn't do things his way, he would vanish again and leave us behind with Mom and all her issues.

"I was so tired. Tired of taking care of Mom, wondering if I'd find her dead from an overdose some night. I was tired of never having enough of anything. I thought the years of dealing with Mom's addiction had earned me the right to the life my father was offering, no matter what his demands were."

He wrings his hands before folding his arms across his chest. "Taking care of me was the least he could do for abandoning me all those years ago. So I came back from Europe senior year and started that prep school and shut myself off from everything and everyone. I barely spoke to my mother, and I talked to Jason even less. I spent every waking moment studying. All I could think about was proving to Cyrus that coming back for me hadn't been a mistake."

His voice cracks under the weight of what he's just said, and his face is pained, as though it too will crack at any moment. But he shakes his head and continues. "I missed you so much, Free, but I thought cutting all contact with you would make it easier for you."

"So what changed? After not talking to me all school year, why call me the night of the accident? Why sleep with mè and let me believe we were back together just to end it a few weeks later?"

"There wasn't a day that went by I didn't want to talk to you. But the night of the accident, I couldn't hold out anymore. There was no one I wanted to talk to more, no one I wanted to *be* with more than you. I was such a mess, Free." He takes a deep breath and continues. "*I* should have been the one in the car with my mother. She was high; she was always high. That night, Jason had to drive all the way down from school to get her. He must have been exhausted."

The mention of Jason and the accident make my stomach churn. "The accident wasn't anyone's fault, though. A deer ran into the road."

He flicks his gaze in my direction. "How do you know that? I didn't find out about the deer until days after the accident."

"Jason told me when he took me on prom night. He told me you stayed by your mom's hospital bed every day until you were sure she'd make it. He also told me that after he was released, you drove him up to the school to get his things."

"Seems like you guys talked about a lot of things."

I nod. "But all we did was talk."

"All night?"

"Seriously, Christopher? You can't really believe I slept with Jason."

He exhales. "No, I don't. But neither of you would talk to me about it, so—"

"So you go straight to 'Free slept with my brother?'" I shake my head.

Christopher shifts, crossing then uncrossing his legs, as though the memories are causing him physical discomfort. "After you ran out of the gym that night, I drove around for a long time. I finally ended up at Cecelia's. I saw Jason's car in the parking lot and the light on in the back."

I open my mouth to protest, but he stops me. "I know nothing happened, but I should have been the one with you, not Jason. I should have pounded on that restaurant door until you let me in, and I'll never forgive myself for not doing that. Instead, I used a fake ID and bought some beer and waited in my car down the block from your house. I must have fallen asleep, and when I woke up that morning, well you know what happened after that."

I take a minute to soak it all in before pressing. "That doesn't explain what happened right after the accident. Things between us seemed okay for a few days. We talked and texted, then all of a sudden, nothing.

Christopher sighs. "When I got back to the hospital, my father had finally arrived from London. He was supportive at first, but even that turned out to be an act. Cyrus is more calculating and devious than any of us could have ever imagined, and the accident gave him the opening he needed."

"Needed for what?"

His tone shifts, the contempt in his voice barely contained. "To keep me in his debt for years."

"How?"

"The hospital bills were going to be astronomical. Mom had no medical insurance. Head injury, physical therapy, occupational therapy, long-term care," he ticks the list off on his fingers. "And the accident tore Jason's ACL. He was a semester away from starting his sophomore year at UG South on a football scholarship. No way he could have stayed at that school without the scholarship." He pauses, then says, "He told you that, too."

I nod.

Christopher continues. "But a couple of phone calls and a few favors later," he waves his hand as if performing a magic trick, "and voilà."

"Cyrus?" I ask.

"Yes. My father is great at calling in markers. The kicker is, he wouldn't have done any of it had it not been for me."

"What do you mean?"

"My mom's medical bills, Jason's tuition, Cyrus didn't

give a damn about them. He hated my mother because he thought she was weak, and Jason hated Cyrus for how he treated Mom, and he didn't do a good job of hiding it back then."

"But Jason works for him now. You both do."

Christopher clenches his jaw. "Old habits die hard. Neither one of us can seem to get out of that man's grasp."

"You said Jason hated Cyrus. Did you?"

He closes his eyes. "I hated the life I had more. Mom's addiction was out of control. At the end of junior year when Cyrus offered to take me in, I jumped at the chance. I even hoped maybe he and I would develop some sort of bond. Turns out taking us in was all about his image. Single fathers who rescue their children from their drug-addicted mothers are heroes. Particularly fathers with political aspirations."

"If Cyrus didn't help them because he cared, why did he do it?"

"My father cares about closing big deals and covering his ass." Christopher gets a faraway look, then adds, "I had no idea the lengths he would go to, the people he would use, just to get what he wants."

He stares off into space for so long, I say his name to get his attention. "Christopher?"

He shakes his head as if turning something loose, then looks at me. "He was working on cementing a deal with Jessica's father. It was the deal that would eventually create CHI and launch my father's development business. In his mind, a merger between the two families—personal and financial—would create a powerful alliance. Cyrus offered to pay for all of it, Mom's medical bills, Jason's tuition, even mine, if I . . ." he trails off.

"Started seeing Jessica again," I finish the sentence for him.

He nods. "The summer before senior year we spent a month cruising through Europe with her family."

My eyes widen at the revelation that while I was back in Pointe Hill heartsick for Christopher, he was cozied up on a cruise with Jessica Riley. Heat rises in my face, and I look away, hoping Christopher mistakes the expression for anger instead of the pain it really is.

"Nothing happened that summer, Free. I swear. Jessica and I didn't start . . ." he searches for the words, but just says, "until senior year."

Although I already knew as much, hearing it still stings.

Christopher must read something in my face, because he says, "I didn't know the two of you had a history. You never told me anything about it. The morning after the prom, it was Jason who told me about the way Jessica had treated you. And he gave me hell for showing up to the prom with her."

On prom night I'd shared with Jason that Jessica had taunted me from middle school all the way through high school. Comments about my appearance, who my parents were and what they did for a living. She rarely said these things directly to me, but always when I was near and always just loud enough for me to hear. Her taunts were subtle, under the radar, nothing to raise the alarm of the adults around us. No fatal wound delivered by a large knife, just a thousand tiny cuts and a thousand tiny scars to show for it.

"What did Jason tell you?" I ask.

"He said she'd treated you horribly in the past. He'd always said you were too good for me. He was right."

"But you came to my house anyway."

He nods. "I came to the house to try to explain. Jessica's father wasn't as cruel as mine, but he was manipulative and demanding, and he had an image to uphold. He expected perfection and that took a toll on Jessica."

"Forgive me if I can't bring myself to feel sorry for her," I say.

He shakes his head, "That's not what I'm trying to do. I just want you to understand some things I'm just beginning to understand myself."

"And *you* have to understand why I don't want to sit in my kitchen talking about Jessica Riley."

He dips his chin, momentarily averting his eyes before looking up again. "I get it. But I want you to know that Jessica and I *never* had what you and I had. Not even close."

I look away because my heart wants to override my brain when he looks at me the way he's looking at me now.

Christopher walks to my small kitchen table and sits. I grab two cold bottles of ginger beer from the fridge and join him. He seems diminished by telling the story. His face is ashen, his pupils pinpricks. I slide one of the beers across the table.

He twists off the cap and takes a long pull. "There's something else I want you to know." Christopher reaches across the table and tries to take my hands, but I ease them away and wrap them around my bottle.

I'm not ready to hear more declarations tonight. Him being here is already sensory overload. We're amped up on memories of the two of us together, and I don't want those memories influencing any decisions we make tonight. So I switch gears.

"Bryan, my *mistake* as you put it, was a director they brought in from out of town to head the project team I'd been assigned to." I stop to take a drink from from my bottle. The ginger burns the back of my throat, and the sensation feels right for what I'm about to say.

"He liked my ideas from the beginning. I was a junior marketing associate, barely at the company a year. Imagine, I'm on a team with a couple of Ivy Leaguers and the director was treating me as though *I* was the star. I was heading up projects, traveling to give presentations. It was good. Really good. And then I started to notice customers posting complaints online, lots of them. Accounts of being lied to, of ending up underwater with the loans they'd received. But Bryan convinced me those were isolated incidents.

"He took me under his wing, shared the company's future plans with me. They would expand into a dozen more states, going into neighborhoods and reaching people other lenders wouldn't touch. He told me I had a bright future with the company, and I believed him. It was one of the few times in my life I saw a future that didn't include the restaurant. Anyway, late-night work sessions between the two of us turned into marathon conversations, and marathon conversations turned into . . ."

I pause, watching a drop of condensation slide slowly down my bottle. "There was a policy against interoffice relationships, so we kept ours a secret. That made it easier for him to lie to me. We never went to his place because he lived near the office. We had take-out at my apartment instead of dining out so our colleagues wouldn't see us together. But he never wore a ring, had no pictures of family on his desk. And I fell for all of it. Stupid, right?"

"Not stupid. Human."

"I wish I could be a little less human sometimes," I say

softly, looking up from my bottle and into Christopher's eyes. I'd seen that look before, and it brings back a memory of us together at school.

We'd been meeting in the library for a couple of months, and Christopher and I had fallen into a routine, sitting across from each other during lunch and the study hall right after. We'd talk quietly from the moment we sat down until Mrs. Berger shushed us, only to get started again the minute her back was turned.

One day the library was unusually busy, the unforgiving Georgia sun bringing students indoors who would normally spend the lunch hour outside in the quads. I waited for Christopher, fidgeting at our table, wondering if the crowded library would change the way he and I interacted.

When he entered, I pretended not to notice how the other students tracked his moves as he approached me. I ignored the smirks, and the questioning glances, and focused on Christopher. He was looking at me as though I was the only other person in the room. When he got to me, he leaned across the table and pressed his lips against mine. It was my first kiss, and so whisper light, I might have thought I'd imagined it, except for the taste of mint that lingered on my lips long after the bell rung at the end of study hall and stayed with me until I fell asleep that night.

I bring my fingers to my lips, and a flush rises up my neck and creeps across my cheeks when I realize Christopher is watching me.

"Did you love him?" he asks, puncturing the silence.

My heart hiccups at the question, but I don't let that show, instead I look out the window at the moon glow coating the wet leaves like a layer of gold paint.

I had dated while I was in college, but Bryan was the

first man I'd been in a real relationship with. The only one since Christopher I'd confessed secrets to. I *had* loved Bryan, even after I'd found out he'd lied. But when I turn away from the window and look at Christopher I don't tell him any of this. I don't say anything at all.

"How did you find out about his wife?" Christopher asks, when it becomes clear I'm not going to answer his previous question.

"We found out about each other. The irony is that it was the only time I had ever been to his place, and I wasn't even alone. Bryan was working from home and had asked another guy on the team to drop some paperwork by. I had something I needed Bryan to look at too, so the guy suggested I tag along. I probably should have come up with a reason not to, but I didn't. I wanted to see where, and how, he lived.

"I knew the moment he answered the door. The look in his eye wasn't surprise or someone pretending to greet a colleague. It was a mix of disappointment and anger. And fear. He let us in, and she was sitting on the couch with her legs tucked beneath her. She smiled and said hello, and I don't know if it was something she saw in my face or Bryan's, but I got called into HR the next day. According to the complaint, I was an overly eager ladder-climber who entered into the relationship so I could receive preferential treatment at the company."

Christopher shakes his head. "What happened to him?"

"The company adored their star director, wouldn't dream of having him taken off the project."

"So they got rid of you."

I nod. "They'd already been unhappy about the emails I'd sent to corporate questioning the things customers were saying about the company. A week later, I got my first write-up about problems with my work." I use air quotes around the word *problems*. "My second and third write-ups happened soon after. The thing with Bryan just made it easier for them to get rid of me."

"I'm sorry, Free."

"A part of me wonders if not knowing would have been better."

Christopher's eyes widen.

"I know how that sounds. They say the truth is always better, but I was happier when I didn't know. I was happier believing everything Bryan said was real. That everything I believed about us was real."

"Maybe it was. Feelings don't know lie from truth." His voice is brittle, as though it's on the verge of breaking again. "But wouldn't you want to know the truth?" he asks.

"If you'd asked me that question before all of that happened, I would have said yes. But the reality is, you can't wrap your arms around the truth in the middle of the night. The truth doesn't keep you company when you're lonely. The truth can't change the past." I shake my head. "I know that's not a very empowering thing to say, but it's how I feel."

Christopher runs his finger around the mouth of his bottle and seems to contemplate my words. "Have you heard from him?"

"He called and texted me for months, emailed me, though I deleted the emails without ever reading any of them. He even sent me a letter a couple of months ago." I look down at my hands. "I read the letter."

"Why?"

"I don't know, I thought reading it might ease my mind."

"Did it?"

I shake my head. The rain starts up again, and I can tell

it's going to be one of those Georgia nights where Mother Nature is as unpredictable as human nature. The rainy night and the easy way we've been talking have started to melt away the wall I'd erected at the beginning of the night. "What did you want to tell me earlier?" I ask.

Christopher averts his eyes and stares out the window I've just turned away from. His look is far away, contemplative, as if the words he needs to say are somewhere outside in the rainy night. "He didn't deserve you," he says, when he looks at me.

The pain in his voice catches me off guard. "No, he didn't, but that's history now."

He leans forward in his chair, "I didn't deserve you either, Free. The thing with Jessica—"

"No more Jessica talk, okay?" I say, raising my hands, palms out. I've heard enough apologies for the night, and each apology only brings up memories I've spent the past seven years trying to forget. "You hungry?"

Christopher blinks, surprised by the abrupt shift in conversation. He studies me for a bit then asks, "You cooking?"

"Cooked. I have leftovers. I own a restaurant; I always have leftovers. I can pop something in the microwave and we can finish going over my ideas."

He doesn't say anything, just stares, and for a second I wonder if I've made a mistake. But then he says, "That would be great."

"I'll meet you out there," I say, tilting my head toward the living room.

I open the refrigerator and grab several containers from the shelves. When I close the fridge door, Christopher is still standing in the doorway. "What?"

He shrugs. "Nothing. I've just missed this."

I raise one of the containers in a mock toast. "To not being enemies."

Christopher raises his bottle. "To almost being friends."

~

TEN MINUTES LATER WE'RE IN THE LIVING ROOM, sitting on the floor with a tray of food on the table in front of us. As we eat, Christopher walks us down memory lane, reminiscing about our past. He remembers everything. From the first day in the library, to the time he burned an entire batch of food at the restaurant trying to help out on a Saturday morning when one of our servers had called in sick.

I turned the television on to provide background noise to fill in any lull in the conversation, but there are none, and soon it's like we're back in high school again, talking like old times. Even when we get tired of talking and focus on the movie instead, the easy comfort is there.

When the movie ends and the credits begin to roll, we both stare straight ahead. The DVD player blinks 1:21 a.m. I'm not tired, though, and Anthony is covering for me in the morning, so I don't have to be at the restaurant early. While I'm wondering what our next move will be, Christopher takes the remote off the table and mutes the television.

I can see his reflection in the screen as the credits roll. He turns to me. I feel the short, hot puffs of breath against my neck, hear his breathing becoming more ragged as he inches closer.

Since he's been back, I've clung to the belief that our attraction is gone, but that belief proves to be a lie when his lips brush the curve of my jaw, right below my earlobe.

"Christopher," I murmur, my voice a raspy mix of demand and desire.

He edges closer, placing his hands on the floor on either side of my thighs. "I've wanted to do this since the day you tossed that box of tissues at my head."

My laugh is cut short when I gasp as he brushes his lips against my ear before gently biting my earlobe. He takes my chin in his hands and turns my head so our noses are almost touching, then presses his forehead against mine muttering my name, over and over, as he kisses my eyelids, then the tip of my nose. When he brushes his face against mine, his stubble rasps against my cheek like a match lighting a fire.

I moan, and Christopher covers my mouth with his, gently at first, then more firmly, until for several minutes, I lose all sense of time and place. Soon, I'm thinking back to the girl I was on the night of the accident, at the restaurant on the couch with Christopher just minutes after he called me, and weeks before a trail of decisions made by others would change our future forever. I pull away.

He's breathing hard and his hair sticks up from where I've run my fingers through it. "What is it?" he asks.

I place my hands on either side of his face and search his eyes for the reflection of the boy I fell in love with. What I see are the eyes of a man whose desire for me has not waned. I pull him into a deep kiss, all the while telling myself that it is just a kiss. A kiss that won't change anything. Then I say it aloud, as if saying it will make it so. "This doesn't change anything, Christopher," I whisper against his lips.

"This," he says, wrapping my braids around his hands and pulling me closer, "changes everything."

CHAPTER TWENTY-ONE

I duck out of the way as the ball whooshes by my head.

"Forty–love!" Iris yells from the other side of the court.

We're playing tennis. Correction—Iris is playing tennis. I'm playing dodgeball. I rub my hip where her last volley landed, then dance on my toes, adopting the beast-mode stance I've seen both Williams sisters take at the height of a match. I'm still trying to perfect the stance when Iris's serve flies by my head.

"Game, set, match!" she yells, running toward me and leaping over the net in one graceful motion.

What I am in the kitchen, Iris is on the tennis court. The only reason I play with her is for the workout I get chasing down her serves. When she saunters over to me, I'm bent at the waist, gasping for air.

"So what's up?" she asks, a grin turning up the corner of her mouth. "Besides me beating you at tennis again, I mean."

I gesture for her to wait until I can catch my breath.

"Nothing really. Things picking up at—restaurant—" I stutter, my lungs burning with the need for air.

Iris stands over me with one hand on her hip and the other bouncing a tennis ball with her racket. Her tennis skirt sways gently around her thighs with every move. "That's cool."

I squint up at her, perspiration stinging my eyes. "Yeah, I tried a new recipe out at breakfast this morning. I think it went over well."

"Great." Iris catches the ball, props the edge of her racket on the ground then leans on it. "Did you try it out this morning before you got to the restaurant, say, on Christopher?"

I spring up like a jack-in-the-box, my burning lungs and thighs all but forgotten. "What . . . how do you—"

"What time did he leave, or is he still there? Did you binge watch *How to Get Away With Murder*? Because if he's rolled up in a rug in your basement, I'll help you get rid of the body."

"He is not rolled up in a . . . how did you know he came to my place, anyway?"

"I was at the corner when the rain started coming down hard again. I figured I'd come back and wait the storm out at your place. I'd just pulled up when I saw him walk up to your door. Imagine my surprise when you let him in." Iris cocks her head toward the bench next to the nets.

We sit, then watch as a couple of guys take the court next to us. Iris puts on her sunglasses and grins at the one who looks like he could be Denzel Washington's son. Denzel Junior is so enamored with Iris he almost walks into his opponent.

"Nothing happened," I say.

"Christopher comes to your apartment and even

though you suspect he might have something to do with that blog post, you let him in. And I *know* you let him stay because you didn't call me last night. So *something* happened."

I prop my elbows on my knees and sigh. "He didn't spend the night, we didn't sleep together, and nothing happened."

Iris tosses me a look over the top of her shades. "Nothing? You might not have slept with him, but don't tell me nothing happened."

I've been dying to blurt it all out since the minute we met for our weekly game. I replay the entire night to her, from the first kiss on the couch, to the kiss he came back for after he'd already started walking to his car.

When I'm done, Iris lets out a long, low whistle. Denzel Junior turns and winks at her, flexing his pecs under his shirt. "Boy, please," she says, under her breath. "You wouldn't know what to do with me if I came with instructions."

I take a sip from my water bottle to hide my laughter. We sit quietly for a while we watch the guys play.

"Look, what you end up doing or not doing with Christopher is up to you."

"I feel a *but* coming," I say, smiling to try to lighten the tension that's seeped its way into Iris's voice.

"But I don't want you to get hurt again."

"I get it, Iris. I do. Letting Christopher back into my life is risky. But it's something I need to do."

"Who said anything about letting him back into your life? So you made out with him last night. He's hot, and the closest you've been to anything that hot in almost a year is the oven at Cecelia's."

I laugh and nudge her with my elbow. "There was that

one guy Mom tried to fix me up with." I shudder at the memory.

"Kermit," we say in unison, using the nickname we'd given the guy after I had described the horror of him leaning in for a kiss at the end of our one and only date. He'd stuck his tongue so far out when he'd moved toward me, images of lizards flicking their tongues had haunted me for days after.

"I get there's a history between the two of you, but I don't know. It all feels too convenient. Too easy."

As if somehow sensing he's the topic of conversation, my phone pings with a text from Christopher.

We're a go 4 meeting w/ Jason Wed.

It's the first time I've heard from him since last night, and a part of me is miffed his text is all business. I'm about to rest the phone down on the bench when another text arrives.

I can't stop thinking about you. When can I see you again?

I glance at Iris, whose eyebrows are cocked. "Is that him?"

"Yeah,"

"And?"

"He's just confirming the meeting with Jason next week." I don't tell her the rest, because despite Iris's cautionary words and my wish that it wasn't so, my pulse still races at the thought of seeing Christopher again.

Iris touches my knee to get my attention. "I just don't know if you should trust him."

"I don't know if I should, either. But if I have to work with him to keep the promises I made to the committee, that's what I'll do. He's set up a meeting with Jason so I can present my ideas about the Old Sixth Ward."

"And what if he wants more, Free? What if this isn't just business to him?"

I don't answer her right away, focusing on the match going on in front of us instead. The hollow thud of the bright, green tennis balls bouncing on the hard court is strangely hypnotic.

"Free?" Iris nudges me.

"What Christopher wants doesn't matter. I'll work with him and I'll do what I set out to do for Cecelia's and for the Old Sixth. I can't handle anything more than that right now."

Iris watches the match in front of us a little longer, and I wait for another warning from her. She props her sunglasses on her head and turns to me. "So, what time are we meeting with them?"

"*We?*"

"You didn't think I'd let you do this alone, did you?"

I had hoped she wouldn't. "Wednesday morning at ten."

Iris tosses her racket in the air, catches it by the handle then stands. "Good. I'll get to your place by nine to help you get ready."

"I don't need your help to get dressed, Iris," I say, certain she's not talking about helping me with my presentation. "I'm not ten years old."

She gives me the once over, "What outfits do you own besides T-shirts, leggings, and that dress I loaned you?"

I twist my lips in thought. "Nine o'clock works."

"Great. Ready for another match?"

I groan. "Seriously? You're just punishing me now."

"Yup. Payback for not telling me about last night right away." Iris grabs my hand and pulls me up from the bench. "By the way," she says, turning and heading for the court, "I was serious about helping you move the body if you needed me to."

I limp onto the court after her. "Yeah, that's what I'm afraid of."

CHAPTER TWENTY-TWO

This time when the elevator door opens on the sixth floor of the CHI offices, I'm ready. I glance at Iris. She's dressed in a tailored suit, her gold loop earrings shimmering under the elevator lights. I smooth my hand over the hips of my charcoal grey sheath dress and take a deep breath as we exit the elevator and make our way to the receptionist.

At the sound of the door opening, a smiling Melissa looks up. Without the shellacked bun, she looks almost friendly. But the friendly smile fades when she realizes it's me.

"Can I help you?" she asks, her gaze darting between Iris and me.

"Melissa, right? I'm here to see Christopher. He's expecting me."

She nods, shifts her attention to the computer screen in front of her, then picks up the phone and taps the keys. "Mr. Eubanks, your ten o'clock is here. Yes, uh-huh, right away." She returns the phone to the cradle then stands. "He'll be right out. May I offer you something to drink?"

"No, I'm fine, thank you," I answer.

"A mimosa would be nice," Iris says.

Melissa looks perplexed and opens her mouth to answer, but Iris cuts her off. "It's a joke, hon. Unless you actually have them on hand, which, in that case, I take mine heavy on the *Mim*, light on the *osa*."

Melissa blinks so fast I think she might be short-circuiting. I tune out the conversation as Iris explains her joke to a clueless Melissa, and turn my head just in time to see Christopher step out of an office and begin heading in my direction. He doesn't see me at first, and the expression on his face is intense, as if he were headed into a meeting with a foe, not a friend.

It's been five days since he came by my apartment, four since he sent the text. When I finally replied, a curt "*See you then*" was all I could manage. I'd finally admitted to myself that his kiss was all I'd thought about since that night. But I sure as hell wasn't about to tell him that.

When Christopher finally notices me, his gaze travels down the length of my body then back up again. The look has the same effect on me as his kiss, and I look away hoping he doesn't notice.

"Free, thanks for coming," Christopher says. The open appraisal he showed as he walked toward me is gone, and now his eyes and voice are all business. "Jason is . . ." he trails off, noticing Iris. "Iris, I wasn't expecting you." He glances at me before returning his attention to her.

"Strength in numbers," she says, in a voice as devoid of emotion as his.

Christopher extends his arm, gesturing down the hallway. "We'll be taking the meeting in Jason's office. This way, please."

The formality in his tone makes me anxious about what to expect from Jason. But it also makes me question everything I thought he and I shared the other night.

When we get to the door at the end of the hall Christopher taps on it once, opens it, then motions for us to follow him into the office. Jason rises as we enter, buttoning his suit jacket and stepping from behind a large mahogany desk.

If there was a contest for looking good in tailored business suits, Christopher and Jason would be neck and neck. I sneak a look at Iris and although she looks unfazed, the way she's gripping the portfolio in her hand tells me she's checking out the Bellamys too.

If Jason is surprised to see Iris, he doesn't let on. "Free, good to see you," he says. The cool, guarded look that was on his face when we entered softens a bit when he takes my hand. "I know Christopher has already explained that we didn't have anything to do with the way that whole blog post thing landed, but I wanted to make sure you heard it from me, too. That wasn't the story we authorized, and we're trying to figure out how the whole thing happened."

I shake his hand and nod.

"Iris," he says, releasing my hand and taking hers. His voice is like dark chocolate when he says her name—smooth but bitter around the edges.

"Jason." She says his name as though she's naming the latest strain of flu.

"Christopher didn't mention you'd be coming."

"He didn't know, but my cousin's BS meter seems to stall whenever she's around a Bellamy. I'm just here to make sure that doesn't happen this time."

Jason holds Iris's hand, and her gaze, for several seconds. I glance at Christopher, wondering if he's noticing the tension between the two of them, too, but his face reveals nothing. Jason finally releases Iris's hand then steps back and gestures toward the table. "Shall we get started?"

Once we're all seated, I pull copies of my proposal from my portfolio and hand one each to Christopher and Jason. "First, thank you for considering this proposal. If you open to the first page, you'll see—"

"Christopher has already filled me in," Jason interrupts, not even glancing at the folder I've placed in front of him. "And frankly, Free, I don't see what's in it for CHI."

I look at Christopher, but his crossed arms and clenched jaw let me know I won't be getting any help from him. "Well, if CHI gets in on the ground floor of a program like this, the benefits to both the company and the community could be enormous. You could position yourself as a company that puts people first."

Jason harrumphs and shakes his head. "In less than an hour, we're scheduled to have a teleconference with our father. If we present this to him," he points at the folder, "with the suggestion that putting people first is the best possible outcome for this company, he'll laugh us out of the room."

"Jason," Christopher admonishes. The brothers stare at each other for a few beats before Christopher continues. "What Jason is trying to say, Free, is that while your proposal is good, we need something more if we want to get the project green lighted."

I had a whole speech ready about the need for Pointe Hill to remain as affordable and diverse as possible, but I now see it won't work on Jason. He is all dollars and cents and ego. So I try another tactic.

"Have you ever heard of Raybones? It's the restaurant in Atlanta famous for its soul food. It's become a destination spot for travelers. Politicians and foreign dignitaries make a point of scheduling photo ops there. Raybones put the south side on the map."

I tap the folder on the table in front of me. "We have the same kind of potential right here in Pointe Hill. Small town feel with urban appeal. I'm proposing branding the merchants in our section of the Old Sixth Ward. We'll call it 'The District' and CHI can be the developer who helps curate it. You'll be seen as the kind of company that helps revitalize communities for the people *already* living there. CHI could help create the model. You'll have representatives from cities all over the country visiting The District to see how we did it. There's money to be made in that."

Jason glances at Christopher then pulls a presentation folder toward him and begins flipping through it. Under the table, I wipe my damp palms on my skirt as Jason studies the proposal.

"And the retailers are on board?" he asks.

"We already have buy-in from some."

He looks up from the folder. "Not all of them?"

"We've only had a couple of meetings, but I'm certain when they realize CHI is working with us, we'll get more."

Iris scoots forward in her chair. "We thought we'd launch the initiative with a kick-off event. An inaugural ribbon cutting ceremony. CHI representatives on stage along with some of the Pointe Hill College students and a few of the merchants, all announcing the initiative and its potential impact on the community. I'll work to help organize the event, and I'm sure I can get Solstice to help as well."

At the mention of Solstice, Jason looks up. "You're familiar with Solstice?"

"I'm one of its senior event planners. Why?"

"I know a few people there. I wasn't aware you worked there, too." He tents his fingers, and taps his bottom lip. "So, all you need from us is to provide program funding."

I glance at Christopher then clear my throat, but he speaks before I have a chance to. "They'll need a good-faith gesture from us, Jason. They need about six months to get the mentor program up and running, find volunteers, and develop the business plan for assisting the merchants who will be a part of The District. During that time we need to allow their original lease agreements to stand."

"Do you know how much money we'll forgo in the short-term by doing that?" Jason asks, eyeing his brother.

Christopher nods. "And I'm thinking about how much we can gain in the long run. No other developer in this area is doing community-centered revitalization."

"And there's a reason nobody's doing it. Cyrus won't want to touch that with a ten-foot pole."

"Maybe that's a good enough reason to consider it," Christopher replies. "We can't keep doing everything that man wants us to do for the rest of our lives." The two stare at each other, neither looking away nor backing down.

"Give us three months to fine-tune the plan and get the mentor program up and running. We can show you mock-ups, marketing plans, websites, all of that by then," I say, breaking the uneasy silence that has settled over the room.

Jason finally looks away from Christopher. He blows out a puff of air then closes the folder and slides it across the table toward me. "You need to get buy-in from more of the retailers. I want to see eighty percent of them signing on within the next ten days. And I want to see a detailed plan and mockups, when you host the event in six weeks."

"Six weeks?" Iris and I ask simultaneously. "We need at least twice that amount of time," I say.

"Six." He turns to Christopher. "After today's call, the next teleconference with Cyrus will be around that time. If you can't help her get this up and running by then, you're the one who has to explain to him why we're not posting higher revenues from those properties." Christopher opens his mouth to speak, but Jason raises a hand to stop him. "And if I don't see the plans, if I don't see any progress within the next few weeks, I won't need Cyrus to pull the plug on all of this, I'll do it myself. And the rents will go back up immediately."

I glance at Iris who lays a reassuring hand on my arm.

"We'll get it done," Christopher says. "I've already talked to a couple of our IT guys and they're willing to volunteer as mentors for the students. I've reached out to several designers I know, as well as a few social-media managers. They've all agreed to help out with the program for at least six months."

Jason nods. "Well, if this goes as well as you seem to think it will, you'll get your bonus, and you'll be able to get out of this place sooner than you'd planned."

"You're leaving Pointe Hill?" I blurt out, before I can think better of asking.

Christopher shoots Jason a look before answering me. "I'm considering it."

I steel my expression, hoping my face doesn't give any hint of the wave of disappointment that washes over me. But Christopher never said he was here to stay, and I admonish myself for hoping he was, even if I hadn't even admitted it to myself until now.

"So, what's the first step?" Jason asks, snapping me out of my momentary melancholy.

I gather the paperwork and begin returning it to my portfolio. "I'll spend some time reviewing the businesses we're targeting for inclusion in The District, then I'll start making calls to set up meetings."

"I'll be accompanying her," Christopher says, surprising me. "I want our tenants to see a face when they think of CHI. I want them to know we're human, too."

Jason stands then walks around the table to where Iris and I are seated. "I'm taking a risk here. Don't disappoint me." He tosses Christopher a look. "You either."

Christopher nods, but he's looking at me when he says, "I'll walk you out."

We step into the hall, and as Christopher closes the door to Jason's office, Iris excuses herself to find the restroom. As soon as she turns the corner, I round on Christopher. "What *was* that in there? You sure were a different guy in that meeting than you were the other night at my place."

"I'd wondered if you even remembered the other night. It's not like you returned my text."

"I did return—"

"Cut the bull, Free. You know what I mean. If you can't even admit you've wanted to see me too, then maybe coming to see you was a mistake."

"Maybe it was. Maybe we just keep it all business from here forward."

We're standing toe-to-toe, and the pull between us is so strong I wonder how we're still vertical. I'm breathing hard, my lungs working as though I've just climbed a flight of stairs. But the only physical exertion I'm doing is working hard not to grab Christopher by his shirt collar and pull him toward me. Whether I'd kiss him or slap him is up for grabs. Until he leans in and whispers, "Tell me you haven't been thinking about me as much as I've been thinking about you. Tell me, and I'll never mention the other night again."

I take in his scent, the same scent I fell asleep with on my lips the night we kissed. He wets his lips. I lean closer, visions of the other night drawing me to him like a magnet. "Christopher—"

"Ready, Free?" Iris calls out from the end of the hall, and I jerk my head back. Sounds penetrate the cocoon that weaves around Christopher and me whenever the two of us are close to each other. A photocopy machine spits out paper, the office's air conditioner hums white noise in the background. Again from Iris, "Free, you coming?"

I turn to leave. But Christopher takes my arm. "We should start visiting the businesses as soon as possible. Are you free this evening?"

"No," I answer, my voice cracking. I clear my throat. "I've got dinner plans." I don't mention that they're with Mom, and the omission gets the reaction I want.

Christopher raises an eyebrow. "Tomorrow, then?"

"Free—" Iris begins.

"I'm coming," I answer, then nod at Christopher before I walk away, fighting the urge to turn around the entire time.

"You okay?" Iris asks when I join her at the elevators.

"Yeah." I press the button to call the elevator although it's already lit. My body's still humming from my encounter with him, and my mind is sifting through the revelation that Christopher might be leaving Pointe Hill. I'm so lost in thought it takes me a few seconds to hear the laughter coming from the end of the hall. I've heard that laugh before. I look down the hallway and see that the laughter is coming from a woman leaning against a cubicle wall, her back to us.

"Free," Iris says when the elevator door opens and she gets on. I'm about to join her when I hear the laugh again.

This time when I look down the hallway, the woman is facing my way.

Danielle.

When she sees me her eyes widen and she takes a step toward me, but I get on the elevator just before the door closes.

~

I END THE CALL AND LAY MY PHONE ON MY DESK. "Christopher says Danielle's an intern, and he hasn't had much interaction with her. I told him I recognized her from coming to the restaurant; I didn't say anything about suspecting she's the one who went to the reporter about me."

Anthony doesn't respond. In fact, he hasn't said much of anything since we got back to the restaurant after leaving CHI's offices. "Just because she's working there doesn't mean anything," he finally says.

"If it doesn't mean anything, why didn't she tell you she'd gotten an internship with them?" Iris asks. She's sitting on the couch next to Anthony and places a hand on his shoulder.

He looks up at me. "I knew she'd applied with a few companies. We hadn't discussed details, I mean it's not like she's my girl or anything. But she knows how I feel about Christopher and CHI."

"She just started the internship. I'm sure she would have told you eventually. But even if she did go to that reporter, how would she know to look into my old job?" I ask.

"Internet research," Iris says. "These days it's not that hard. Anyone looking for dirt on anyone else can find it."

"Well, Christopher is going to talk to the reporter. She's been out of town. We'll know more when she returns," I say.

Anthony sighs and fiddles with the hearing aid wire running behind his ear. "You think her giving me her number, agreeing to go out with me, was all about getting dirt on you? If she'd really wanted this internship, someone at CHI might have rewarded her for bringing this information about you to them."

Iris says, "I know they both denied it, Free, but I'm not sure it's a safe bet to rule either Christopher or Jason out. They are the ones who'd stand to benefit the most from getting you off that committee and out of the way."

"I don't know," I say, sitting on the couch next to Anthony.

"I have to go, I've got class," he says, looking up at the clock on the wall before getting up and heading to the door. "Free, do me a favor? Don't say anything to Christopher about suspecting Danielle, not yet anyway. I don't want her to lose the internship. I want to talk to her first."

"Sure," I say.

Iris grabs her purse. "I'll walk out with you." She gives me a peck on the cheek. "I have to get back to the office. Simone is still making a fuss about me missing the meeting the night of your chamber event. Send some positive vibes my way."

After they leave, I head to the office and begin sorting through some paperwork, but it's a waste of time because the only thing I can focus on are my encounters with Christopher over the past few weeks. First at his office, then his house, then at mine. And now today after the meeting.

Every time we've seen each other there's been arguing and tension, and attraction so heavy, it has mass. I told Iris I couldn't handle the thought of having anything with

Christopher, but after today, I realize something *is* happening, whether I think I can handle it or not.

CHAPTER TWENTY-THREE

"Try deepening that green and moving the oval over a bit to the right. It's still not quite there," I say, peering over the shoulder of the college freshman eagerly working on updating a logo design for one of the Old Sixth Ward merchants.

I leave her, walking around the room and observing the dozen or so students set up at various workstations. The computers, large-screen monitors, and software they're working on have all been donated by CHI. I was nervous about how involved CHI would be in this project, but in the three weeks since our meeting, they've stepped up in a big way.

All but four of the two-dozen businesses we've been working with have signed up to participate in the program. Christopher has never missed a meeting with the merchants, and any anxiety I had about his ability to relate to the business owners fizzled after our first couple of meetings with them. Christopher was charming, respectful, and approachable, listening to their concerns and offering valuable feedback.

Things between the two of us were awkward at first, as we navigated the boundaries of our new dynamic. We hadn't had another hot and heavy make out session, but the air between us was heavy with the weight of things I suspected we both wanted to say and do.

After the first week of meetings, I gave up the pretense that seeing him every day was a chore. During week two, when we stopped for gelato on the way to meet a couple of vendors, I reluctantly admitted I was enjoying his company. And this past weekend, when we walked shoulder-to-shoulder through the crowds attending Pointe Hill's Labor Day Book Fair, I had to fight against the instinct to take his hand. Christopher Bellamy has been on his best behavior. But C. J. Eubanks is still in there somewhere, and I'm not sure who will ultimately win out.

I shake thoughts of Christopher out of my head and lean against the doorway, watching the volunteers interact with the students.

My muscles tense when I sense him come up behind me, but I keep my eyes trained on the students in the room, not turning or acknowledging his presence. He stands behind me quietly for several seconds before saying, "They're doing a great job. You all are."

After a long day at the restaurant and several hours here at the school, Christopher's voice is like a massage—warm and soothing, working out some of the tension in my shoulders.

"They're doing a great job, thanks in part to CHI." I turn and look up at him, "And you." He smiles, and the smile begins to loosen the tension further down my body. I look away before the smile makes me say something I'll regret. "The shop owners are happy with what they've seen so far, and the students have been learning a lot. There's already a waiting list for the spring session."

"Yeah, Danielle mentioned."

Danielle has helped coordinate the CHI volunteer schedule. She's denied being the one who went to the *Post* with my information, explaining that she kept the internship a secret because she knew how Anthony felt about Christopher. I'm inclined to believe her, but Anthony still seems skeptical. In the absence of any proof against her, Christopher allowed her to keep her internship.

"Can we talk outside?" Christopher asks.

I motion for him to follow me through a side door, and we exit the building and step into the warm September evening. Dusk paints streaks of orange and pink against the sky's blue canvas, and a chorus of night-calling insects seems to applaud the sight. Christopher and I lean against the side of the building until he breaks the silence.

"Danielle is still insisting she's not the one who gave Vanessa the information for the blog post, and I believe her."

"If she didn't, who did?"

"Vanessa's not saying, but . . ." he trails off.

"What is it?"

Christopher bends his leg and props his foot against the wall behind him. "Jason and Simone have a history."

"Simone? Iris's boss?"

"Yeah. He says he mentioned our past together and talked about CHI's plans for the Old Sixth Ward. Still, he doesn't think she'd go to the press with the information."

"But you do."

"Simone and Jason's relationship—if you can call it that —is volatile. Sometimes they act like they hate each other, other times I wonder what they wouldn't do for each other.

Solstice is linked with CHI, and when we do well, they do well. Maybe Simone thought she was helping him out."

"Helping herself out is more like it." I'm sure Iris isn't aware of any relationship between Simone and Jason. I'm wondering how much more Simone knows about Christopher and me when he interrupts my thoughts.

"I meant what I said in that text."

"What text?"

Christopher grins, his eyes glinting in the evening light. "The text you ignored the night after I came to your place."

I tuck my hands in my pockets and pretend to focus on the sky. Anything to avoid looking into those eyes. "I should have said more in my reply, I just didn't know what to say. Everything I typed seemed to be too much and not enough." I finally look at him and my heart catches in my throat when he pushes away from the wall and faces me.

"Free, I was hoping maybe—"

"Ms. Spalding?" The student I was working with earlier sticks her head out the door and motions for me to return to the room. "I made some changes to the logo, and I'd like you to take a look."

"Do you mind?" I ask Christopher, grateful for the interruption.

"I'd love to see what she's done."

Inside, we stand behind the student's workstation and view the variations she's come up with.

"Impressive," Christopher says, nodding.

He asks the student questions about her creative process and points out the things he likes most about each treatment. He's supportive and positive, yet provides helpful feedback. It's a side of him I've not seen before. When another student asks for my assistance, I leave them and make my way across the room, spending a few minutes helping the student with some web content she's developing.

My phone vibrates in my pocket and I grab it and read the text.

You should go out with me.

I look up, and Christopher is across the room staring at his phone, a grin on his face.

I smile and tap in a quick response. *Who is this?*

I hear Christopher chuckle, but I don't look up from my phone.

The last man you kissed.

Billy? I reply quickly, and this time everyone in the room hears Christopher's laugh.

Go out with me. Please. It's all I've been thinking about.

I finally look up from my phone. The grin is gone from Christopher's face, and he's watching me intently. I start texting him back when a phone call comes through. I hold up a finger to alert him that I'm taking a call, then turn to answer.

It's Mrs. Foster calling to tell me that Mr. Foster has had an allergic reaction to something he ate earlier. He'll be okay, but they're on the way to urgent care. The high school student who works for her has to leave in twenty minutes, and she can't get ahold of her daughter to close up the store. She asks if I'd mind closing up for her. I assure her it's no problem and end the call, filling Christopher in on the details.

"Mind if I come with you?" Christopher asks as I grab my bag and head out the door.

I smile. "Not one to miss out on an opportunity for free ice cream, huh?"

"That, and depending on how you answer my text, this might be the closest I get to going out on a date with you."

CHAPTER TWENTY-FOUR

An hour after I've locked up for the Fosters, Christopher and I head back to his office to prepare for an early-morning meeting.

While he drives I throw discreet glances in his direction, watching the way the lights from the cars behind us reflect off the rear view mirror and onto his face. When he glances my way and catches me looking at him, he takes a hand off the steering wheel and gently strokes a finger across my cheek. I'm grateful for the music playing in the car, because I think I might have actually purred.

The heat between us cools somewhat once we get to his office and start working. We work quietly for about an hour, only stopping once when Christopher orders Chinese food. When the office's motion sensor lights flicker off after a period of inactivity, I laugh when Christopher flails his hands to reactivate them.

"I've missed that laugh," he says, standing and stretching.

From beneath hooded eyes, I watch the muscles in Christopher's arms tighten as he stretches them above his head. The hem of his untucked shirt rises, revealing a thin trail of hair below his navel.

Suddenly, I'm aware of a tightness in my own body. I rub the sore muscles in my neck then rest the papers I'm holding onto the table and walk over to the window to distract myself. In the distance, houselights twinkle against the backdrop of the night sky.

Christopher joins me at the window. "You didn't answer my question."

His nearness ratchets up the tension in my body. "What question?" I barely squeak out.

He shifts, resting his hands on my waist, then leans forward so his mouth is close to my ear. "Go out on a date with me."

His breath against my ear short-circuits the list of reasons I'd been compiling in my head about why going out with him would be a bad idea. But he doesn't wait for an answer before snaking his hand under my arm and resting it against my stomach, drawing me closer. "We've got seven years of dates to catch up on."

When he leans in to kiss my neck, I roll out of his embrace. "Don't leave Pointe Hill." I regret the words the minute they leave my mouth. It's an admission that I want him here, and I'm embarrassed I made it. I don't wait for a response before walking back to the chair.

Christopher pulls up a chair and sits across from me, so close his knees touch mine. "I spend a lot of time traveling for CHI, especially to New York and London. It makes sense to look for something in either, or both, of those places."

I look down at my hands and start picking at a hangnail.

"But if I thought there was something more for me here in Pointe Hill, I'd find a way to work things out so I could be here more often, maybe even all the time." When I'm silent, he leans in. "Do you know the first time I saw you?"

"The library. You plopped down across from me like you belonged there."

He chuckles. "No, that was the first conversation we ever had, but I'd seen you before. You'd been walking down the hall completely immersed in a book you were reading. But when I walked by you looked up at me. It was just for a second."

"I don't remember that."

"And I'll never forget it. For days after, I hoped to catch glimpses of you in the hall, but I never saw you again. Then one day it dawned on me, books, library." He laughs. "And of course, that's where I found you."

"You came looking for me?"

He makes a motion crossing his heart. "Scout's honor." He places his hand on the nape of my neck and pulls me closer. "I think I was looking for you before I even knew who you were."

I wrap my fingers around his forearms, and when he leans in and kisses me it's like we pick up right where we left off the other night.

"Billy ever kiss you like that?"

"Billy who?" I murmur, through my smile.

Christopher pulls me up, and when we're both standing, moves with me until the backs of my legs hit his desk. I splay my fingers across the desktop, seeking purchase against the glass surface.

He lowers his head until his lips graze the bare skin above the V-neck of my T-shirt. "Your heart is racing," he says, the bass in his voice vibrating through my body.

I lay my palm flat against his chest. "So is yours."

When we kiss again, the coarse hairs on his cheek rasp

against my face, magnifying my awareness of skin against skin. I allow the sensation to quiet my mind and temporarily shut off any questions I still have about us.

Christopher grips my waist, lifts me, then lowers me onto the desk. I gasp and arch my back against the cold glass, and Christopher moans, lowering his head and trailing kisses through my shirt down the length of my body. He nudges up the bottom of my shirt with his nose, and when the damp heat of his lips touches my bare stomach, I jolt and tug at his hair.

"Ticklish?" he murmurs, nibbling at the spot just above my navel.

"Ticklish isn't the right word," I sputter.

He straightens, balancing his weight on his arms and hovering above me.

"What are you thinking?"

His lips quirk up in a smile before he bends to kiss me as he deftly undoes the top button of my jeans.

"I was wondering how many times I could—"

"Call from Lucky Panda." Siri's voice blurts an interruption through Christopher's phone.

We both freeze, our heavy breathing amplified in the quiet office.

"Call from Lucky Panda," Siri repeats.

"Stupid app," he groans, staring at me but not moving. The phone quiets after the third notification.

I'm about to pull him in for another kiss, when the lights click off. I've almost managed to stifle the laugh threatening to erupt when Siri announces, "Call from Lucky Panda."

I dissolve in a fit of laughter.

Christopher moans. "Shit."

I shrug. "I *am* hungry."

He shakes his head slowly and glances over my body. "So am I."

"Call from Lucky Panda," Siri says again.

Christopher straightens, and I prop myself up on my elbows. He gives me a look that's full of regret, then heads to the table to take the call. "This better be some damn good Chinese food."

By the time Christopher returns with the takeout, my breathing and body temperature have almost returned to normal. I'm back at the table and have moved the papers to make room for dinner.

Christopher looks disappointed when he sees everything has returned to normal. "I guess we're having dinner now."

"You said you were hungry," I say, smiling, as he sits and begins unpacking the takeout bag, handing me a pair of chopsticks and a box of lo mein.

"It's probably for the best, anyway."

I stop with the chopsticks midair, a noodle dangling from it. "And why is that?"

"It's been years since I've seen you, and although we've been spending a lot of time together, we technically haven't had a date. We should probably do that before," he gestures toward his desk, "all of that."

"We've had takeout together a couple of times since we started the project," I say, laughing.

"I mean a real date. An 'I ask you out and pick you up at your place' date."

He places his food on the table and rests his elbows on his knees. "So, Free, would you go out on a date with me?"

The sixteen-year-old Free inside me is doing pirouettes. The twenty-four-year-old Free nudges her over and joins her. I put my takeout box on the table and face him, mirroring his pose, resting my elbows on my knees. "Christopher Bellamy, I would love to go out on a date with you."

———————

CHAPTER TWENTY-FIVE

"Why the change of heart?" I ask, watching as Iris throws clothes from my closet onto my bed.

She pauses and I think she's going to answer me, but she holds up a pair of faded denim overalls instead. "Do you even try, Free? I should make you wear this on your date with Christopher just to punish you."

Christopher and I had planned on having our date before tonight, but in the weeks since that evening in his office, we've both been working around the clock to prepare for the District launch event tomorrow.

"I swear, looking at this closet you wouldn't know we're related," Iris says, flipping through the clothes in my closet like she's the host on an extreme makeover show.

I throw a pillow at her. "Shut up."

"Wait, what do we have here?" Iris pulls out a dress from the back of the closet and tears the clear protective plastic off. It's an ankara print with a fitted top and slightly flared skirt that hits just above the knee. Its vibrant purple and yellow pattern and deep V-neck are a far cry from my usual outfits.

"This is *definitely* something I'd wear," Iris says, holding the dress up and posing in front of the mirror. "Did I lend you this?"

While the dress looks just like something Iris would wear, it's mine. I'd bought it when Bryan and I had made plans to go away together for the weekend. I was excited about not having to hide our relationship from colleagues and splurged on the dress. But he'd canceled at the last minute, and the dress never made it out of its protective bag.

"No, I bought it." She gives me a surprised look, but doesn't ask any questions. "Well, it goes perfectly with the earrings I brought. When we put your hair up, Christopher won't know what hit him."

I hop off the bed and walk over to her, trailing my fingers along the fabric. "It's too dressy. We're just going to dinner."

"Did you see the suits he and Jason were wearing at that meeting? The Christopher you remember may have been a burger with a side of fries kind of guy, but he's not that anymore. You're not going to a burger joint, trust me on that." Iris places the hanger over my head, allowing the dress to drape in front of me.

I admire the dress in the mirror, tilting my head and imagining Christopher's reaction when he sees me in it. "Okay, I'll wear it."

Iris literally jumps for joy, grabs her purse then motions for me to follow her to the bathroom. "Sit," she says, once we're both crammed into the small space.

I position myself on the bathroom stool as Iris rummages through her purse and pulls out a makeup bag the size of a small carry-on.

"I don't want—" I begin, but she's already applying lip liner before I have a chance to finish. I give up, and move to another line of questioning. "You never answered me. A few weeks ago, you were warning me about letting Christopher back into my life. Now you're applying my makeup and practically feeding me birth control pills in preparation for my date with him. What's up with that?"

Iris leans in, using a makeup sponge to blot my cheeks. "I've watched him over the past few weeks. He seems committed to the project. Maybe he's changed. Aunt Agnes told me he came by the restaurant one afternoon last week after you'd already left for the day."

Mom had told me Christopher had come by the restaurant to express his condolences for the loss of my father. She told me he apologized for how he treated me on prom night and for showing up drunk to the house the morning after.

When I'd asked Mom how she had responded to him, she'd said, "He asked for forgiveness, and it was in my power to grant it to him, so I did."

Iris shrugs. "If you and your mom can forgive him, then I guess I can, too. Maybe the Bellamys aren't as alike as I thought."

"What's the deal with you and Jason? I saw the way you looked at each other at the meeting."

Even though she doesn't answer, her nose flares just enough for me to know I'm right in suspecting the two have some kind of history.

"Close your eyes," she says.

I close them and she begins applying shadow to my eyelids.

"There is no deal. We just don't like each other very much."

"Is that all?"

"Yup. So, you ever hear back from that woman about the job in DC?"

I raise a brow, knowing there must be more to the Iris and Jason story, but decide to drop the topic for now. "Her name is Carmen. She's called a couple of times and sent me emails outlining the responsibilities of the position."

"You considering it?"

"Not seriously, not right now anyway. But it would be a chance to help more communities. Maybe make up for what I did at Berry & Barlow."

"Hey," Iris says, placing her finger under my chin and tilting my face up so I'm looking into her eyes. "You didn't do anything wrong at that company. You don't owe anyone anything."

I nod, but a part of me still feels guilty. Guilty about working for an organization that hurt many families and guilty for being in a relationship that might have ruined one.

Iris works on my makeup in silence for several minutes then steps back and rests her hands on my shoulder. "You look beautiful. I mean, you always look beautiful, but *this*, this is good. See for yourself."

I turn on the stool and face the mirror. Iris has given my eyes a smoky look that accentuates their almond shape, and she's picked the perfect shade of lipstick for my skin tone. I blow out a deep breath.

"Relax," she says. "It's only a date."

"It feels like more. It's like a long time ago I pressed pause on a movie I was really into. And now it's been so long, I don't know if I'll remember all the reasons I enjoyed it before the break, or if the end will live up to my expectations."

"So use tonight to remember the things you loved, and then decide how fast or how slow you want the rest to go by."

"How'd you get so smart, cuz?" I ask, hugging her.

"Experience," she says, laughing.

Twenty minutes later I'm in front of the full-length mirror in my bedroom looking like a million bucks, when the doorbell rings, startling us. We both jump, then giggle like a couple of teenagers.

"Sounds like your date is here," Iris says, grinning.

I walk to the front door and open it, beaming. But it's not Christopher standing there. Instead, it's an older man dressed in a black suit and tie.

"Ms. Spalding?" he asks.

"Yes?"

"I'm Derrick, Mr. Bellamy's driver. He's been delayed, and he's instructed me to take you to meet him."

The disappointment must show on my face because Derrick says, "Mr. Bellamy asked me to relay his apologies and his sincere promise that he'll make it up to you later."

My nerves are on edge as I get into the car, but Derrick talks to me as he drives, and his talking helps calm my nerves. He explains that he owns a fleet of cars, and that he has driven the Eubanks family around since the boys were in high school. He glances up at me through the rearview mirror. "He's told me a lot about you, and he doesn't talk about much." Derrick smiles then returns his attention to the road.

I have a ton of questions for him, starting with what Christopher has said about me. But I don't have time to ask because Derrick slows the car, then I hear gravel skipping under the car's tires. I press the button to roll the window down and look outside. We're in the driveway of Christopher's old house. "I thought I was meeting him at his office."

Derrick winks. "No, but I'm sure he's been working hard just the same. Enjoy your evening, Ms. Spalding."

CHAPTER TWENTY-SIX

I step out of the car just as a soft autumn breeze rustles the leaves in the trees and teases the hem of my dress. I look down, holding the material against my thigh, and when I look up, Christopher is standing on the front porch. He's wearing a black V-neck sweater and slim-cut gray slacks, his hands clasped in front of him.

I barely hear Derrick drive off as I approach the porch, walking up the stairs and holding the railing tightly to steady my nerves. Christopher takes my hand at the top of the stairs and plants a delicate kiss on my wrist. "Mmm," he says, inhaling deeply, "you smell as amazing as you look."

"I thought you were working late," is all I can manage in reply.

"I was, but not at the office." He takes my hand then opens the screen door and leads me inside. I step into the foyer, and the first thing I notice is the smell. "You've been cooking?"

He breaks into an easy smile and shrugs. "Trying to. I thought I'd given myself enough time, but I haven't done this in a long time, and I had things in the oven and couldn't leave them." He glances over his shoulder toward the kitchen. "Will you give me a minute? I'll be right back."

While he heads down the hall, I look around the foyer and notice that the floors have been stripped and sanded, the walls painted.

He returns and hands me a glass of wine. "You decided not to tear the house down after all?" I ask before taking a sip.

Christopher nods. "It's a beautiful old house. It's worth saving. I never brought you here when we were younger because of all the memories it held. Who knows, maybe one day I'll get the chance to make happier memories here."

Suddenly things feel like they're going too fast, so I slow them down by bringing the conversation around to the thing that grounds me. "So, you really cooked?"

Christopher smiles and places his hand on the small of my back. He guides me to a small circular table in the center of the living room. A lace cloth drapes the table, a candle flickers in front of two place settings.

He looks sheepish. "I wanted to do something to show you that the way I treated you back then, and the way I behaved when you came to my office, they're things I've done. But this, working to make this place the home it never was, being there for you over the past few weeks, cooking for you tonight, is who I am. Who I want to be."

This is the Christopher I remember. The one before his father, before C. J. Eubanks, before everything that complicated us. This is the man I fell for. "I've missed this Christopher," I say softly.

He kisses me then pulls out my chair, motioning for me to sit. "I'll be right back with your first course."

When he returns, he places two small salads on the table and joins me.

"Thank you. This is perfect."

He takes my hands in his. "I want us to try again, Free. I'm here and I'm going to make things right. Back then, I was too afraid of what I'd lose if I stood up to my father, and I ended up losing the most important person in my life. I won't make that mistake again." Candlelight flickers between us as he leans across the table and kisses me softly on my lips.

I do most of the talking throughout our meal of almond-ricotta tortellini with truffle butter. I tell him about college and my life before moving back to Pointe Hill. I talk about my time at Berry & Barlow, about my relationship with Mom, then and now. "I'm sorry, I'm hogging the conversation," I say when I realize I've been talking nonstop for almost an hour.

He smiles. "I want to hear everything."

"But what about you, your life in London? Your travels to New York?"

He takes a sip of wine then studies his glass. "Things didn't work out the way I'd imagined."

"Is that good or bad?"

"Not all bad." He tilts his glass and watches the wine roll toward the edges. "After all, it brought me back here to you." He looks into the distance for a moment before asking, "Do you still have that necklace I gave you?"

I chuckle. "I wore that thing so much it got rusty."

"It was all I could afford back when I gave it to you."

"I know, and it meant everything to me."

"You were wearing it the night you came over after the accident."

I nod and although I haven't worn the necklace in years, I brush my fingers along my chest where the locket once sat.

"That night, I told you I felt like I was hanging on by my

fingertips, remember?"

Tears well at the back of my eyes as I recall the night. "And I told you to let go. And I promised to catch you when you fall."

"I believed you, Free. I believed it then, and I believe it now. There have always been so many things getting between us. And there are things about my father and my family I have to tell you. But just for tonight, just this once, I want it to be about you and me."

I swipe away a tear then raise my glass. "To you and me."

"To us," he says. Christopher kisses me on the forehead while I dab at my eyes with my napkin. "You ready for dessert?"

We share a bowl of rum raisin ice cream on the couch, and the cold rum flavor melding with the warmth of his tongue make for a dessert unlike anything I've ever had before.

"Show me around," I say after we've emptied the bowl.

Christopher takes me on a tour of the house, walking me through the kitchen, an office and a small bedroom and bathroom at the back of the house. Then he stops in front of the only door we have not entered.

"Your bedroom?"

He nods, and I enter the room. Christopher leans against the doorframe while I look around. The space is as modern and sparsely decorated as his office. The king-size bed has a dark gray comforter pulled taut over the mattress. A single end table sits on one side of the bed, the lamp atop it softly lighting the room. Across from the bed, two small closets bookend a fireplace, and a door on the opposite wall leads to a master bathroom.

I walk past the bed, running my fingers along the plush

comforter, then peek into the bathroom. The dark granite countertop is clutter free. Stylistically, C. J. and Christopher aren't that far apart. I return to the bedroom and look at Christopher. He's still standing in the doorway, his body framed by the hall light behind him that masks the expression on his face. I'm glad I can't see his eyes because it makes it easier to say the things I'm about to say.

"It took me ten years, but I'm finally inside Christopher Bellamy's bedroom." I try to deliver the line with a trace of humor, but if Christopher picks up on it, he doesn't react. He remains perfectly still.

"I lied about the thoughts I had about you in your room," I say, the admission causing my skin to warm.

"What did you think about?" His voice slides over me like silk, raising goose bumps all over my body.

"I thought about what it would feel like to run my hands over your body." I step out of one of my heels.

"What else did you think about?"

I step out of the other shoe. "I imagined what it would be like to be with you." I glance over at his bed, "In your bed all night, waking up next to you in the morning."

Christopher shuts the door behind him. "Come here, Free."

I go to him and when I'm standing right in front of him, he takes me by the waist and turns me so I'm facing the door. He presses his body against mine, and I gasp at the sudden movement.

His voice is raspy in my ear. He slips his leg between my parted thighs and presses even harder as he trails kisses down the back of my neck. "Did you imagine this?"

"Yes," I answer, breathily. "A thousand times, yes."

Christopher turns me so we're facing each other. "After tonight, you'll never have to rely on your imagination again.

~

THE ROOM IS DARK, EXCEPT FOR THE LIGHT SEEPING IN from under his bathroom door. I turn, trying not to wake Christopher. He shifts, curling his arm around me and pulling me closer, but his breathing quickly returns to the soft, rhythmic sound of deep sleep.

Last night was a lifetime away from the night we spent together as teenagers. The night of the accident we'd made love on the couch in the office at Cecelia's. But there'd been no time for basking in the afterglow, no time to fall asleep in each other's arms. Christopher had to get back to the hospital, and I had to get back home.

He'd driven me home, parking a block away from my house so my parents wouldn't see his car. We'd shared a teary goodbye, unsure if we'd be able to see each other over the next few days. He'd texted me when he got back to the hospital to tell me he loved me. And we'd spoken the next morning, making plans to see each other in a few days when he was sure his mother was out of the woods and when his father wasn't breathing down his neck.

But his mother's recovery was slow. After a few more texts and the call explaining that with his mom's condition still serious, he wouldn't be going to the prom, the next time I saw him was when he showed up at the prom with Jessica.

My chest tightens at the memory, but, as if sensing the tension in my body, Christopher pulls me closer. "I got you," he murmurs, his heartbeat a slow, steady drum against my back. "I got you."

I match my breathing to his so that our chests rise and fall in unison, and images from last night begin running through my head like a playlist. His fingers raking through my hair, my hands gripping his. Our breathing, growing louder and more ragged as the night progressed.

I turn and face him and trace the outline of his lips with my finger. He moans my name, and the sound licks against my body like a flame. I kiss him and he darts his tongue out, deepening the kiss. Soon, I no longer need to rely on the images from last night. Christopher creates a whole new playlist, even more exquisite than the night before.

There is no heavy warmth next to me when I wake up this time, and for a split second, fear replaces bliss. But then I hear the shower running in the bathroom, and I smile at my silliness, sliding beneath the covers, allowing the blissful feeling to return to me as if it were my birthright.

I've almost drifted back to sleep when Christopher walks into the bedroom with a towel wrapped around his waist. In that hazy space between sleep and wake, I watch him walk to one of the closets and open the door. He rummages around for a few seconds then pulls something out of the closet, closes his fist around it, then grabs his pants from the floor and pulls them on.

"Hey," I say.

He turns, and a wide smile spreads across his face. He sits on the edge of the bed and kisses me. "Did I wake you?"

"I woke up while you were in the shower."

"Been admiring me this whole time?"

"The whole time," I answer, smiling.

He kisses me again, a deep, satisfying kiss that makes me want to tug him back into bed. But he pulls away then reaches a hand into his pocket. "Free—"

A faint buzzing sound comes from the bedside table, and Christopher frowns then grabs his cell phone and checks the screen. "It's Jason. It might be about this evening. I'll make it quick."

"Hey," he says, smiling at me and running his hand along my arm as he listens to the call. After a minute, he turns away, but I see his smile falter before he does. His tanned back, still damp from his shower, hunches slightly. A minute later he says, "I'll be there in a few."

The smile is back when he turns to me, but his hand is empty. Whatever he was holding is back in his pocket.

"Hey," I wrap my arms around his shoulders. "Everything okay?"

He kisses my forehead. "I'd planned on having breakfast here with you before heading out, but something's come up."

"What is it?"

He looks away anxiously, but his expression is calm when he looks at me again. "CHI stuff."

"Anything to do with the event?"

"Nothing I can't handle. Jason and I will take care of it before the event kicks off, I promise. I don't want you worrying about anything." He takes my hands and kisses my fingertips before pressing my palm against his face. "I wish I didn't have to go, but I'll have Derrick pick you up whenever you're ready. If it wasn't urgent—"

"I understand. Besides, I've got a ton to do to get ready for later."

Christopher toys with the sheet around my waist. "After we get through tonight, I want to talk to you about our future."

"Our future. I like the way that sounds."

"Me too."

He heads to the bathroom, and I flop back in the bed, wondering if that call and the thing in his pocket have anything to do with our future.

CHAPTER TWENTY-SEVEN

A balmy breeze blows across Magnolia Street, rustling the glossy, leathery leaves of the trees that give the street its name. The banner stretched across the street between two lanterns flaps above my head as if dancing to the music blaring through the large speakers. Merchant booths line the sidewalks on both sides of the street as crowds sample merchant wares at the Old Sixth Ward District Initiative.

I watch Iris weave her way through the crowd, her hand clasped around a megaphone she's been toting around all day like a weapon, keeping rambunctious teens in order. The merchants all seem pleased. The Fosters sold out of inventory an hour ago, Mr. Makao has said he's expecting to sell out soon, and we only have a couple of trays of food left, and there's still a line at our booth where Anthony and my mother have been working all day. By all accounts, the event has been a success.

I've been here since leaving Christopher's house this morning, and there were flowers waiting for me when I arrived at Cecelia's. But after a quick conversation to thank him, I haven't had a chance to speak to him since. I've spent much of the day shuttling between Cecelia's kitchen on one end of Magnolia and our vendor booth on the other end, close to the makeshift stage. By the time I get a few minutes to check my phone, I realize I've missed several texts and calls from him. I'm about to return his call when Mom walks over with an empty serving dish.

"We're out of chicken. There should be a batch keeping warm in the oven. That should take us through the evening." She wipes her forehead with the back of her arm and looks around, taking in the busy street. "You did a wonderful job with all of this, Free. I'm very proud of you. Your father would have been, too." She rests a hand on my cheek, "You look happy, honey."

Her words cause a hitch in my throat, and I look away and around the crowded street. I *am* happy. Happy the event is a success, happy because it looks as if Cecelia's will be around for a long time, and I'm happy Christopher is back in my life.

I roll the cart back to the restaurant, loading the large chafing dish of chicken onto it. I call Christopher before heading back out, but my call goes straight to voicemail. By the time I get back to the booth, the music has been lowered, and the crowd's talking has dimmed to a low hum. I squeeze in between Anthony and Iris and follow their gazes to the stage. As twilight sets in, Melissa crosses the stage.

"Free, hold the tray steady," Mom cautions.

My focus flicking between the dish and the stage, I lean against the table and angle the chafing dish so mom can transfer the contents to the waiting containers.

Melissa is all smiles as she begins speaking, but Jason, who's just emerged and stands off to her left, doesn't share her enthusiasm. His face looks strained, his eyes periodically shifting to something off stage.

"Hey, everyone, my name is Melissa Charter, and on behalf of CHI and The District Initiative, I'd like to thank y'all for coming out today and helping us make our inaugural event a hit."

Melissa bobs her head as applause ripples through the crowd. "Before I introduce the team behind this evening's event, I'd like to bring out a special guest. It's been tough keeping this one under wraps for the past couple of weeks, but—" she lets out a delighted shriek and tosses her hair, "I did!" Melissa moves to the side and extends her arm to an area off stage. "Ladies and gentlemen, please join me in welcoming, Cronus Holdings' Founder and CEO, Cyrus Eubanks." The crowd applauds again and Melissa bobs and clasps her hands as though she's just introduced the Queen of England.

Cyrus Eubanks struts onto the stage. He's taller than both his sons, his silver hair cut stylishly low. He's wearing glasses with tinted lenses, and although he's older than I'd imagined, looking at him is like looking at what I imagine Christopher will look like in forty years.

Melissa looks up adoringly at the older Eubanks as she hands him the mike.

"Her enthusiasm for him extends beyond basic employer appreciation, don't you think?" Iris whispers, but I'm too focused on the stage to respond.

Cyrus works the stage like a politician, waving and greeting the crowd with an affable, down-home manner. Jason is smiling now, but his tightly clasped hands and the way he keeps clenching and unclenching his jaw tell me he's not happy to see his father. And then it dawns on me— this is what Jason called to tell Christopher this morning.

Cyrus takes the mike from Melissa. "Thank you. It's a pleasure to be here in Pointe Hill again. It's been far too long. I have always said that family and community are the most important things in the world, so I'm honored to be here to help kick-off our initiative."

Iris and I exchange glances. "*Our*? He had nothing to do with any of this," I hiss under my breath.

"My sons have worked hard over the past several weeks, and the work they've done is a great first step, but tonight I'm excited to announce that this is just the beginning. In a matter of weeks, CHI will officially launch phase two of this initiative, and we are in talks with corporate sponsors who will help give The District a more high-end feel."

"*High end*? That's not what the District is supposed to be about. That's not what this initiative is for," I say.

"These corporate sponsors will ensure we'll be able to bring residents and tenants to Pointe Hill who will help put it on the map as one of the trendiest spots south of Atlanta."

"Free, what is he talking about?" Mom asks.

"I don't know. This isn't what we discussed with Christopher and Jason." I slide the chafing dish onto the table and pull my phone out of my apron pocket to call Christopher. The signal is weak, and the call indicator spins and spins as it tries to connect.

On stage, Cyrus motions for Jason to come closer then cups a hand above his eyes and scans the crowd. "My other son, Christopher, is here somewhere. I'm fortunate to have my boys in my life now. I missed out on their early years. It was something my father had done to me, and I had promised myself I would be different. But I allowed ambition and other circumstances to keep me from them. It's something I will always regret. After the tragic accident that hospitalized their mother," he squeezes Jason's shoulder, then takes a deep breath before continuing. "I was fortunate to be able to step up in a way I hadn't had the opportunity to when they were younger. Not only as a father to them, but as a grandfather to my grandson, Shayne."

"Grandson? I didn't know Jason had a son," I say.

"Neither did I," Iris says, her eyes laser focused on the stage.

Cyrus motions to someone off to his left, and the crowd near the steps leading up to the stage parts to let through whoever he's motioning to.

I see the hair first. Auburn and perfectly styled into a neat shoulder-length bob. Jessica.

Cyrus takes her hand and helps her onto the stage. I spread my fingers across the front of my shirt kneading my chest as if somehow that will loosen the tightness gripping it. When I'm finally able to take a breath, I see who's walking on stage behind Jessica. A young, auburn-haired boy with eyes the same vivid green as Christopher's.

CHAPTER TWENTY-EIGHT

The boy, who looks to be about six years old, walks on stage, his emerald eyes twinkling, and waves to the crowd.

"Oh my God," Iris says, placing a hand on my arm.

"Christopher has a son?" Anthony says.

Even though we're outside, I feel like the walls are closing in on me. I close my eyes and struggle to fill my lungs with air, pressing my hand against my chest as though applying pressure to an open wound.

The voices on stage sound like they're coming from inside a tunnel, but snippets of the conversation filter through the pounding in my head. "My daughter-in-law and CHI's new head of acquisitions . . ." And from Jessica, "Came straight here from the airport . . . excited about my new role . . ."

I back away from the table, and somehow snag the plastic tablecloth as I do. The chafing dish crashes to the pavement. The metal clanging against the ground sounds distant and warbled as if it's happening to someone else, somewhere else. Gravy from the dish splatters and large drops of the hot liquid hit my hand, burning my skin.

"Free!" Mom's voice pulls me out of the tunnel and back to the present, and the first thing I see is Christopher rushing toward me. His eyes, larger, sadder versions of the boy's, pull me all the way back to reality and to the heat rolling across my hand.

"Mom . . ." I groan.

"Bring me a towel!" Mom yells. Seconds later I feel a cold cloth being wrapped around my hand. Around me, people are talking, but I can't make sense of their words. My eyes are locked on Christopher, who's pushing people aside to get to me. I shake my head over and over again as he approaches.

He's only a few feet away when Anthony yells, "Stay the hell away from her!" and steps between Christopher and me. Iris is yelling too, and in the commotion, I turn my back on all of them and start running.

I snake my way through the crowd and run until the pain in my lungs surpasses the one in my hand. I run until the night air grows cooler and until twilight turns to dusk. But no matter how far or how long I run, nothing eases the burning in my heart.

I DON'T KNOW HOW LONG I'VE BEEN RUNNING OR HOW far I've run, but at some point I end up back at the restaurant. When I open the back door, Mom, Iris, and Anthony are in the kitchen.

"Thank God," Mom says, rushing up and pulling me into a hug. When I flinch, she steps back and gingerly removes the towel wrapped around my hand. "It's not blistering, but maybe we should have it looked at just the same."

"I'm fine," I say, dropping the towel onto the counter and taking a fresh one from a stack on the counter. Anthony takes the towel from me, and after running cold water over it, gently rewraps my hand. "You didn't know?" he asks. "About Jessica or the kid?"

I'm afraid if I speak I'll start crying again, so I shake my head and walk back to the office. Mom and Iris join me on the couch, flanking me like a pair of protective bookends, while Anthony paces in front of us, gnawing on his nails. "What do you want me to do?" he asks.

"What you did was a good start," Iris says.

"What did you do?" I ask.

"He threw a punch at Christopher. Would have landed it too if Jason hadn't pushed Christopher out of the way first," Iris answers.

"Is she in there?" Christopher's voice booms from the front of the restaurant.

I jump up from the couch as he comes barreling through the swinging door, followed closely by Jason.

"Free, I need to talk you," Christopher pleads.

"Talk to Free my ass," Iris says, rushing from the office and walking right up to him. He towers over her, but she doesn't flinch.

Anthony moves to her side. "You have some nerve coming here."

Christopher raises his arms, palms up. "I don't want to hurt you, Anthony—"

"Hurt me?" Anthony chest bumps Christopher, but Jason steps between them before things can escalate.

"The last thing any of us need right now is more

drama," Jason says, pushing his brother back toward the door.

"Jessica and I aren't married anymore! We went to the justice of the peace when we were both nineteen. It didn't even last a year before we got it annulled." The words tumble from Christopher's mouth as Jason tries to pull him back.

"That's a technicality!" I say as I enter the kitchen. "You made it sound like what the two of you had was insignificant. But you *married* her, your father refers to her as his daughter-in-law, and you have a child with her! *A child*! We've spent almost every day together over the past few weeks, and you didn't tell me any of this. I can't believe I fell for your lies again. I'm so stupid . . ." My voice breaks, and I turn to walk away, but there's something else I need to know. "How old is he?"

Christopher swallows hard. "I tried to tell you so many times . . ."

"*How old is he?*"

"He's seven. But—"

"She was pregnant when you brought her to the prom. Is that why I never heard from you after that?"

"I didn't know she was pregnant."

I keep shaking my head, and I'm starting to feel dizzy, so I move over to a stool and sit.

"Please, Free, can we just talk somewhere, alone? Please, give me a chance to explain."

"Are you serious? Get the hell out of here, Christopher," Iris begins before Jason interrupts her.

"I think we should let them talk in private," he says, calmly. "It's time everything came out in the open."

Iris's eyes widen. "You're such a hypocrite. You want to get the secrets out in the open? Does Christopher know—"

"Iris," I say, sharply.

Christopher looks at Jason. "What is she talking about?"

Jason glances at me, frowning. I look away, my head too full from what I've learned today to care that I revealed his secrets. He shakes his head then glares at Iris before answering Christopher. "Nothing that's any of her business," he says, before looking at Iris again. "You need to learn to stay in your lane."

"I'll stay in my lane when your family stops wreaking havoc in mine."

Jason ignores Iris's remark and grabs his brother's arm, but Christopher shakes loose.

"I didn't know they'd be there tonight. Cyrus did this, all of it." Christopher speaks in starts and stops, his words strained. "There are things you don't understand. Things I'll explain."

"Are you and Jessica—" I've barely begun asking the question when he answers.

"Not anymore. Not for a long time." Christopher closes his eyes. "You are the one I wanted to be with, the one I still want to be with. Please, Free, can we go somewhere and talk? I can't do this here."

"I don't care about what you can and can't do. I don't care why you did what you did, or why you came to my house the morning after. I care that you lied to me again. And that you've been lying to me since the day we met. You didn't choose me back in high school. The truth is . . ."

The truth sits bitter and hot at the back of my throat like cerasee tea, and I spit it out so it doesn't choke me. "The truth is, you settled for me. Jessica is the person who fits the kind of life you've always wanted. Your suits, your car, your corner office." I get up from the couch and run my hands across my apron before opening my arms wide. "This is who

I am, Christopher. I'm the girl with the stained fingers, wearing the apron and the T-shirts, and Converse sneakers. You don't *really* want that. You never did."

Christopher's face crumples. "Don't you dare say that. Don't you ever say I don't love you just the way you are. I always have."

You could hear a pin drop in the silence that follows. No one says a word as Christopher and I stare at each other from opposite sides of the counter. I don't back down, I don't look away. And when he finally does, I say, "I want you to leave, now. You don't belong here."

Christopher opens and closes his mouth several times, but doesn't say anything before turning and walking out. Jason lingers a moment longer, watching me before turning his steely gaze on Iris. Then he leaves, too.

I stare at the kitchen door for a long time. Long after I hear the chime of the front door closing behind Christopher and Jason. Long after Mom tells Anthony and Iris they can go. I stare at the door until my tears are so heavy, the only way to find relief is to close my eyes and let the tears fall.

CHAPTER TWENTY-NINE

Mom is in the kitchen making tea, and I'm lying on the couch looking at the office through my tired, puffy eyes. A large, old painting of Jamaica's Hope Gardens takes up much of the wall across from the couch. Folders and paperwork are scattered across the desk, and squeezed in among the envelopes and bills is a flag-set holding miniaturized versions of both the American and Jamaican flags.

The flag-set is a twenty-year-old flea market find my dad insisted on keeping long after the colors of both flags had faded. I lost count of the number of times I'd walked into the office and caught my father admiring it as though it was a family portrait. The memory of my Dad with the flags triggers another memory.

Mom, Dad, and I were in the kitchen at Cecelia's. It was after Dad's stroke, and he'd been recovering at home, but was still too weak to help. So he just sat on a chair by the counter, wearing his apron and listening to Mom and me jabber on.

At one point, Mom was telling a story about her and my aunt getting into trouble when they were kids, and I looked over at Dad. We had both heard the story a hundred times, but Dad was grinning as if it was his first time hearing it. His mustache needed trimming, and his whiskers curled down over the corners of his mouth.

When he looked over at me, he placed his hands over his heart and smiled his signature smile that reached all the way to his eyes. The next day he was back in the hospital. A week later, he was gone.

A few days after he died, Mom and I were back at the restaurant, and I saw his apron lying on the chair where he'd left it. I put it on and made the first batch of tarts I'd ever made without him. Mom and I ate them together, our sniffling and the clinking of our forks against our plates the only breaks in the silence.

Later when Mom gathered the linens to do the laundry, I didn't add Dad's apron to the wash. I rolled it up and hid it on a shelf at the top of the closet, instead.

In a flash, I'm on my feet pulling open the door to the linen closet. I stand on my toes and splay my fingers across the top shelf, frantically searching for the apron. My fingers graze soft dishcloths and crisp linen napkins, but not the stiff canvas material of Dad's old apron. In a panic, I start pulling things off the shelf, wondering if despite my care in hiding it, Mom washed it.

Dishcloths flutter by me onto the floor, creating a small pile at my feet. My heart pounds and a fresh round of tears prick at the back of my eyes. When my fingertips brush the familiar rough canvas of the apron, the tears break free. I pull the apron down and bring it to my face as I collapse onto the pile of dishcloths. The apron smells a little like the fabric softener sheets Mom keeps in the closet, and a little like caked on grease and cinnamon, but mostly it smells like Dad. I bow my head and weep into the scratchy material.

I don't know how long I've been sitting like that, when I feel Mom's arms around me. "Shh, honey, it will be alright," she says in my ear, while holding and rocking with me.

"I was embarrassed by him," I sputter.

"Embarrassed by who?" Mom asks, softly.

"Daddy," I begin, but the pain of the memory starts a fresh flow of tears that leave me gulping for air.

"Breathe, honey, just breathe."

I take a deep breath and continue. "He came to the school when I was in the fifth grade. I'd forgotten my lunch." I pull out of her embrace and look into her eyes. "He was wearing the apron, and I could tell he'd come straight from the restaurant. I could smell the food on him . . . he was so happy when he saw me at my locker. And then he saw the look on my face."

My words come in gasps and spasms as I try to catch my breath between sobs. "Oh, Mom, I just didn't want the other kids to tease me. I didn't mean to hurt him." I collapse into her arms again, crying even harder. "I didn't mean to hurt him. I tried to make it up to him. I helped him with his party that weekend. I was working so hard, that's when I cut my hand . . . I came back here to help you both. I wanted to fix things. Make it right. I know what it feels like when someone you love looks at you the way I looked at Daddy that day. I felt it on prom night. I felt it with Bryan. I wish I could go back in time and change that day. I wish Daddy knew how much I loved him."

Mom wipes away my tears with the edges of the apron, then pulls me up tightly against her. Her body is shaking, and she's crying too. "He never doubted your love for him, Free. I promise you. You don't know this, but years ago, before your dad got sick, we got an offer to sell this place. They were offering a good sum of money, too."

I look up, wiping my eyes. "Why didn't you take it?"

"Because your dad wanted this restaurant to be your future. He wanted it to be his legacy to you, if you wanted it."

"And what do you want for me?"

She pauses for a while, then says, "Remember when I told you that when I was younger all I wanted was to be happy? How I thought my happy would mean traveling the world? I had it in my mind that there was only one way to be happy. That my happiness would take this one, predestined shape."

"And now?"

"Your dad created a new shape for the happiness to fill. Then when I had you, that shape changed again. Free, you have to figure out what that shape looks like for you. It wasn't up to your father, and it's not up to me. It's not up to the people on that committee or in Pointe Hill. And it's not up to Christopher."

I nod, and she smiles, wiping away her own tears. "Did I ever tell you how you got your name?"

I chuckle. "Once or twice, but you can tell me again."

My mom starts in on the familiar story and I listen, huddled with her on the floor of the linen closet, the old apron squeezed into the space between us.

CHAPTER THIRTY

One minute I'm warm under my blanket, the next, a blast of cool air assaults my body. I splay my fingers across my bed, feeling around until my hand touches the soft blanket I must have kicked off in the middle of the night. My fingers don't make contact with the blanket, but I do locate a couple of cheese curls I somehow missed during last night's snack-food binge. I pop them into my mouth without even opening my eyes, then, like a turtle retreating under its shell, tuck my head and arms into my pajama top.

"You have until the count of five to get up or this glass of water is going to end up all over your head."

I scream and sit straight up in the bed.

Iris is standing above me, a glass of water tilted over my head. I've never regretted giving Iris a key to my apartment before, but there's a first time for everything. I blink at her, then groan, my head pounding from a seventy-two hour chocolate and cheese-curl fueled Netflix marathon.

"I'm serious, Free. Up. Now."

"Okay, okay." I shoot her a look that would wilt mere mortals. Iris just tilts the glass further.

I pull my arms out of my pajama tops, and as she rests the glass on my bedside table I give her the universal one-finger symbol for *thanks, but no thanks.*

"Aunt Agnes told me you smashed your phone the other night. I figured I'd give you until today to stop feeling sorry for yourself." She walks back to me and lets out a low whistle.

"Don't say it." After the weekend I've had, I don't need to see myself in the mirror to know how awful I look.

"Have you had a decent meal since yesterday?"

"Chocolate," I answer, nodding.

Iris reaches over and pulls something out of my hair. "And cheese curls."

I grab the cheese curl and shove it in my mouth. Iris has seen me do worse. Iris has done worse. I pull my knees up to my chest and wrap my arms around them.

"Scoot over," she says, toeing off her shoes and climbing into bed next to me. We sit silently with our backs against the headboard until I rest my head on her shoulder.

"What's this?" She reaches down to the end of the bed and picks up an old shoebox. The box is full of pictures of me as a baby, many with either Mom or Dad at my side. There's a tiny stuffed animal, a barrette a friend brought me back from Jamaica, and other assorted baubles.

Iris rummages through, then holds up a necklace. Its chain is broken and knotted, and little spots of rust mar the fake silver. A tarnished, book-shaped locket hangs from the chain. "What's this?"

I take it from her and toss it in the trash. "Something I should have thrown out a long time ago."

Iris slides the box onto the floor, then lowers her body so she's lying on her side. I do the same, until we're face-to-face on the bed. "You know, you're not the only one who's not sure about what they're doing. I'm in debt up to my eyeballs."

"What? But your car, the condo, your clothes . . ."

"Debt, debt, debt."

"Can you ask your parents for help?"

"Probably . . . maybe. I'll find a way to figure it out, and that's why I'm telling you this. I want you to know you're not the only one who doesn't have it all together, but you'll figure it out."

I pick at a corner of the blanket. "I don't know what I'm going to do about anything. About the restaurant or Christopher."

"The event was a hit, though. People are still talking about it. And regardless of what Cyrus said, there's no way CHI could try to raise your rent right now."

"It's not just about that. Jessica's back in Pointe Hill with Christopher's son, and he's renovating his old house. When I first realized that's what he was doing, I thought maybe he was thinking he and I would start a family there. But now . . . the thought of seeing them together all over town . . ." I shake my head.

"He said they weren't a couple."

"I know what he said, but why should I trust anything that comes out of his mouth? Would you?"

"I don't know, Free. I know I'm the one who cautioned you about getting involved with him, but there was some-thing about him the night of the event. I saw his face when he realized Jessica and his son were on stage and that you'd seen them. He looked devastated. I don't know, I think you should talk to him."

"What could he say that would change any of it?" I reach over to the bedside table and hand Iris a business card. It's smudged with cheese powder but you can still make out Carmen's name.

Iris sits up straighter. "Are you thinking about taking the job in DC?"

"She's calling me on Friday."

"You'd leave Pointe Hill?"

"I don't know. But like you said, CHI won't raise the rent anytime soon. The restaurant is doing better than it ever has." I take the card from Iris and study it. "Maybe my happy means leaving Pointe Hill again."

Iris is quiet for several beats before saying, "Well, you don't have to make a decision today. Why don't you hop in the shower, and I'll order us some food. Then we'll figure out where to go from there, okay?"

As Iris heads into the living room, I take one last look at the card before shuffling to the bathroom, hoping a long, hot shower will do the trick and help clear some of the fog in my head.

It feels good to let the shower's warm water wash away the funk I've been in for the past three days. As I'm toweling off, I hear the doorbell ring, and like Pavlov's dog, the sound triggers my hunger. I yank my robe on and head out to the living room.

"I hope you ordered Chinese food, I'm . . ."

My hunger vanishes when I walk into the room to find a haggard looking Jason sitting on my couch. He stands when I walk in.

"What is he doing here?"

"Don't be angry," Iris says. "He called me and asked if he could come talk to you."

"And you told him he could?"

"I think you need to hear what he has to say."

I stare at her incredulously before turning to Jason.

"We're going to extend the old lease terms for the businesses in the District, and it wouldn't have happened if it wasn't for all your hard work," he says.

"That's great, but you didn't have to come here to tell me that."

"I know, but there's more you need to know."

I flick my gaze toward Iris. She nods, and I motion for Jason to sit.

He takes a seat on the couch and begins right away. "Neither Christopher nor I had any idea Cyrus was in town. We didn't find out until that afternoon."

"But you called Christopher," I say, remembering the phone call that had erased the smile from Christopher's face.

Jason nods. "Yes. Someone from the London office called to ask when Cyrus was due to arrive in Pointe Hill. I called Christopher to find out if he knew anything. He didn't and we weren't sure about any of it until Cyrus turned up at the office that afternoon. But even then he didn't say anything about Jessica and Shayne or this phase two plan he dropped on us at the event."

"Shayne," I say, as it dawns on me I'm hearing the boy's name for the first time.

"Christopher tried calling you, but he couldn't get you. He was on his way to look for you when he found out Jessica and Shayne were flying in and were on their way to the event. He raced to get back before they did, but by the time he got back, Cyrus was already on stage. Christopher wasn't on stage with me because he was backstage pleading with Jessica not to go out there.

"There are things I'm just now learning, Free. You have to talk to Christopher, please. We're both tired of all the secrets." Jason leans forward in his seat and scrubs a hand across his face. "I told him I'd taken uppers the night of the accident."

I pull my robe tighter and take the seat across from Jason.

"Mom had a DUI record a mile long, and Christopher and I had sworn to each other we'd never drive under the influence of anything. I was too ashamed to tell him I was high when I got behind the wheel. I told Cyrus, though, and somehow he got the tox results thrown out. You were the only other person who knew about it. But I didn't realize Christopher was keeping secrets from that night, too."

"What secrets?"

"The night of the accident, Mom called Christopher."

"From the hospital? How? He told me she'd been unconscious when they brought her in."

Jason shakes his head. "She'd called him earlier that night. At least a half dozen times."

"And when she couldn't get him, she called you?" Iris asks, taking a seat on the sofa's arm.

Jason shakes his head again. "No, she called a cab to take her to Christopher's school. But when the RA told him that a woman who was claiming to be his mother was downstairs in the lobby acting weird, Christopher knew she was high again, and he told the RA he didn't know who the woman was."

I sink back into the chair. "That's why he feels so guilty about the accident."

"The only person he told was Cyrus, and our father has used our secrets to keep us at odds with each other and in debt to him all these years. It's how he got us to work for him. It's how Christopher got so involved with Jessica in the first place."

"Whoa," Iris says, softly. "That's some heavy stuff."

Jason hesitates, then stands walks to the door. "Talk to him, Free. He'll tell you everything. About Shayne, about Jessica, Cyrus. Everything. He's at the house if you decide to go see him."

CHAPTER THIRTY-ONE

E xcept for a small light coming through the living room window, the house is dark when I pull the truck behind Christopher's car in the driveway.

In typical Georgia fashion, the temperature has dropped considerably, and an autumn wind wraps its cold fingers around me. I get out of the truck and pull the collar of my cable sweater up around my ears. My hand is still a little sore from the burns, and a dull ache throbs just below the surface.

I take the stairs slowly, practicing my speech in my head, but I hesitate near the top. I think about what my mom said about finding my happy and question whether learning the truth about Christopher's past with Jessica would bring me closer or farther away from it.

I think about Carmen's business card on my nightstand and about making a fresh start somewhere else. Somewhere where no one knows me, where the only expectations I'll have are the ones I place on myself. I'm about to return to the truck, ready to leave the past few months behind, when I hear the dull clunk of a bottle tapping against wood.

"Come to save me from myself, Free?"

I look up and Christopher is perched on the wooden railing at the far end of the porch, one leg planted on the floor, the other stretched on the rail in front of him.

"How long have you been out here?" I ask, pulling my sweater around me and eyeing his thin T-shirt.

"Long enough to see that you really don't want to be here."

I walk over to the railing, and lean against it, too far to touch him, but close enough to notice the goose bumps on his arm.

He tilts his head toward my hand. "How is it?"

"It'll be okay." I tuck my still-bandaged hand under my arm.

He studies my face for several seconds then raises the bottle he's holding. "To the end of things."

"The end of what things?"

"The end of lies and liars. The end of me working for Cyrus Eubanks. The end of us."

His eyes are bloodshot, his face unshaven. I don't know what I expected, but this angry, barely sober man isn't it.

"We ended a long time ago," I say.

He laughs humorlessly. "You're almost as good a liar as I am."

"Jason told me about the night of the accident."

He hesitates before taking a pull from his beer bottle. "So Jason sent you here." He drains the bottle then rests it on the floor. It tips over, clinking against the empties already there. "And you've come to say goodbye. Well, goodbye, Free. Have a great life."

"That's it? You drop a bombshell on me then tell me to have a great life?" I push off the railing and tilt my head toward the pile of empties on the floor. "Keep that up and you're going to end up just like your mother."

"I can take care of myself," he barks.

"God I hate you sometimes."

I head toward the stairs, but Christopher steps in front of me so quickly, I almost crash into him. "I'm sorry, Free. It's cold out here; please come inside and we can finish talking in there."

I shake my head. "We *are* finished." I run down the stairs, my truck a blur from the tears stinging my eyes.

"Free!" Christopher calls out from behind me.

I run the last few feet to the truck and grab the door handle, flinging it open and hopping in. I already have the key in the ignition when Christopher plants himself between the door and the truck and stops me from closing the door.

"I'm sorry, Free."

"I'm sick and tired of hearing how sorry you are. You promised me you and Jessica never had anything like we had. First at my place, then at yours." I try to push him away, but he doesn't budge.

"I meant everything I said. There has only ever been you here, in my heart." He beats his hand against his chest. "I promise you."

"You have a child with her!" I turn the key in the ignition and try to pull the door closed.

"Free . . ."

"No, Christopher, just let me go. Please, just let me go."

"He isn't mine."

I blink at him, slowly releasing my grip on the door. "What?"

"Shayne is not my son."

CHAPTER THIRTY-TWO

T he truck's open-door warning chimes as I stare at him. "But his eyes . . ."

Christopher reaches inside the truck and removes the key from the ignition. "Are green like mine and like my father's. Shayne is my half brother, not my son."

I sit in stunned silence as the realization dawns on me. "Your father and *Jessica*?"

"I didn't know about any of it until four months ago, just before I came back to Pointe Hill."

A gust of wind blows through, and I pull my sweater around my shoulders. Christopher takes my elbow. "Come inside, please."

We walk to the house in silence, my hands still shaking from the shock of what I've just heard. Inside the living room, a couch and coffee table occupy the space where we'd sat down to dinner just a few days ago. The silver picture frame is still the only thing on the fireplace mantel. I sit at one end of the couch, and Christopher sits at the other, as if he needs as much space to tell his story as I need to hear it.

"Jessica and I *were* married, but what I told you the

other night is true. It lasted less than a year. We got married when we found out she was pregnant. Her father is old-school South. Very old-school. No way he was having an unwed mother for a daughter."

Christopher picks up his bottle to take a drink, but just stares at it before putting it back down. "We shouldn't have married. Not for that reason. I guess I thought somehow we could make it work."

"Why didn't it?"

"Our relationship was built on fear and desperation. We were both trying to please our fathers, and I was still trying to get over losing you. It was doomed from the start."

"How did you find out Shayne wasn't your biological son?"

"Jessica and I have joint custody. A few months ago while she was traveling out of the country, he got really sick and I rushed him to the hospital. Turned out his appendix had burst. While I was filling out the pre-op paperwork I saw his blood type. I know my blood type, and I know Jessica's."

Christopher glances at the bottle on the table again then stares at his empty hands, bending then flexing his fingers. "Shayne is left-handed like me," he says, smiling. "When I talked to the nurse at the hospital and tried to tell her there was some kind of mix-up, she told me I must have gotten my blood type wrong. I mean, anyone could look at Shayne and me and see we were related, right? But by then, I'd already figured it out.

"Jessica rushed back to New York that night, and when I confronted her she broke down and told me everything. She'd known from the start Shayne wasn't mine. We'd been on-again, off-again during our senior year. On the night of the accident, we hadn't seen each other for a couple of months. It was during that time that she and Cyrus . . ." he trails off.

"I can't believe your father would do something like that. You're his son. And Jessica was only seventeen, for God's sake."

"And Cyrus was a fifty-four-year-old business owner who showered her with gifts and promises of a future together. He made her think he really cared about her."

"He groomed her."

Christopher nods. "And it wasn't illegal. Georgia's age of consent is sixteen. The man is despicable, but he's no fool."

"How long did it last?"

"Jessica said it only lasted for a couple of months before Cyrus ended it."

"Cyrus was the one who ended it?"

"Yeah, but not because he'd suddenly grown a conscience. He'd gotten what he wanted. I'm sure he got tired of her. I think he did the same to my mother. She never talked about him, but I'd hear her on the phone with Cyrus when I was a kid. She'd be crying, pleading with him, apologizing. For what, I never knew."

He tilts his head toward the picture on the mantel. "That's the only time I remember him being around. The worst part is, I blamed my mother. I thought Cyrus left because she was such a mess. It's why I jumped at the chance to go live with him back in high school. Why I went to work for him after college. But he has an evil streak in him. He rarely talks about his own dad, but I think his father must have hurt him badly."

Christopher touches the side of his mouth with his finger. "He's got this scar right here. I asked him once how he got it and all he said was, 'I didn't answer my old man fast enough.' But instead of being better than his father, Cyrus was worse. My mother was probably not the first woman he used, and I'm sure Jessica wasn't the last. So when Jessica realized she was pregnant and wanted to keep the baby, she knew she couldn't tell Cyrus he was the father."

"So she got back together with you."

"That night when I asked you to the prom, Jessica and I hadn't been together for a while. She'd been with Cyrus during that time, but after the accident, he ended things with her. I think him pushing Jessica and me back together was his way of getting her out of his hair. And he could come off looking like a saint by paying Jason's and my mom's medical bills. By the time prom rolled around, Jessica knew she was pregnant, but she knew it couldn't have been mine. I was a wreck after prom, and then when your dad said you never wanted to see me again, I went to see her, and we . . ." he trails off, shaking his head.

"That didn't take very long," I say, shaking my head.

Christopher swipes a hand across his face. "I was hurting, Free. That's an explanation, not an excuse. I was still in love with you, and I shouldn't have slept with her. I know I screwed up."

"So when Jessica said you were the father, you had no reason to doubt it."

"None. Her family invited me to spend another summer with them in Europe, and we were together during that time, too. She didn't start showing until her fifth month. Shayne came early, but he was small, and he looked just like me. There was never any reason to suspect anything."

"Cyrus never questioned it?"

"Jessica lied to all of us about how far along she was.

Swore to him it couldn't be his. And he was all too willing to believe her."

"Who else knows?"

"I told Jason when I came back to Pointe Hill, but that's it. Cyrus doesn't know, and we can't tell him. I can't let him do to Shayne what he did to Jason and me. I don't know what he'd do if he knew."

"And what about Shayne?"

"He's only seven. How can we tell him I'm his brother and his grandfather is really his father?"

"*You* are his father, the only one he knows. The only one that matters."

Christopher nods, then looks around the living room. "Jason asking me to come back to Pointe Hill when he did was perfect timing. It was a couple of weeks after Shayne got out of the hospital. We'd always planned for him to spend the summer in London with Jessica's parents. He went there, and I came here to try to figure things out."

"Have you?"

"Some things. This is the longest Shayne and I have ever been apart. I miss him so much, Free. The thought of him not being a part of my life—" Christopher breaks off abruptly and swallows hard. He's bouncing his knee in a quick, jerky motion, and I reach out and still it with my hand. He studies my hand on his knee for a few beats before continuing. "I'm not confused about my feelings for Shayne or my feelings for you."

Christopher reaches down and takes my hand. "That day when you came here to confront me about the inspection at Cecelia's, I saw how angry you were with me, and it was the first time I'd felt hopeful since I learned the truth about Shayne. I convinced myself that a part of you still cared. You wouldn't have gotten so angry if you didn't remember what we had been, if you didn't miss what we once were. You made me want to try to fix things. This house, my relationship with you. I thought if I fixed this place up, maybe there was a chance you and I could start over. Try again."

"What about you and Jessica?"

"There *is* no me and Jessica."

"You have a child with her. There will *always* be a you and Jessica. She won't just let you move back to Pointe Hill with her son." I sit back against the couch, putting space between us again. "And if you're thinking of moving back here just because of me, you shouldn't. I've been offered an opportunity to work in DC."

Christopher jerks his head up. "DC? You're moving to DC?"

"Maybe it's for the best."

"What about Cecelia's? Your mom, the Old Sixth?"

"The position in DC would mean helping out a lot more communities like this one, dozens of places like Cecelia's."

Christopher stands abruptly and walks over to the fireplace. "I don't want you to go. I know that's selfish, but it's true. Shayne, this house, and you are the only things in my life I'm certain of."

He returns to the couch and stoops in front of me. "The night of the chamber meeting, I tried to tell you everything, and then I tried a dozen times after that. I was going to tell you the morning of the District launch event, but then Jason called and everything happened so fast. I'm sorry I kept this from you, Free. *So sorry.* I was a mess when I got to Pointe Hill. A sad, angry mess. But being with you these past few weeks, I see glimpses of who I can be. Who I *want* to be." He sits next to me on the couch then takes my hands in his.

"But I want you to be happy, and if that means you leaving Pointe Hill, then as much as it hurts me, I won't try to stop you."

I look down at our joined hands. "I don't know what I'm going to do yet."

"Whatever you decide, however long you're here for, let me be there for you. Whether it's a couple days or weeks or months, I just want to spend time with you. No parents, no interference, just you and me."

"I don't know if I know how to move forward. I don't know how to make it so everything here in Pointe Hill doesn't remind me of our past together. I don't know how to forget."

Christopher cradles my face in his hands, his expression hopeful and sincere. "We'll help each other. I started by repairing this house, erasing the bad and trying to replace it with something good. You and I already made a pretty good memory here."

I chuckle. "We did."

"Don't give up on me, Free," he pleads. "Don't give up on us."

He pulls me closer. I curl up against his side and lay my head on his chest. His heart is beating quickly, and his pulse pounds against my ear. We sit quietly and I listen as his breathing eases and his heartbeat slows. I feel drained of all energy, too tired to think about making any decisions. So I close my eyes and match my breathing to his. As I teeter on the edge between wakefulness and sleep, Christopher kisses the top of my head then whispers, "I got you, Free, I got you."

CHAPTER THIRTY-THREE

I t's been three weeks since Christopher asked for a do-over, and in those three weeks, we've seen each other almost every day. Late lunches at Cecelia's, milkshakes at Foster's, and we've even had dinner with Mom and Sam. Christopher has brought Shayne for Sunday brunch at Cecelia's a couple of times. Watching the two of them together, it's clear how much they love each other, and it's helped me see Christopher in a whole new light. He's genuinely happy when he's with Shayne, and I see none of the worry or pain I saw in his eyes the night he revealed his secret to me.

Today when I glance up at those green eyes, they're filled with anxiety. Christopher, Jason, and I are seated at a conference table waiting for two additional people to arrive before our meeting begins. I glance at Jason, and he looks as anxious as Christopher. I know what they're planning, and if I was about to do what they were, I'd be anxious, too.

A rap on the door gets our attention, and Melissa pops her head in, announcing Cyrus's arrival. She's almost giddy when he walks by her in the doorway, and he doesn't even try to hide his ogling as he watches her walk away.

Cyrus seems surprised to see me in the room, but the look quickly vanishes, and is replaced with the charm I witnessed while he was on stage at the event. "Ms. Spalding," he says smiling, "what a pleasure." He glances at his sons. "Although I thought this meeting was just a formality. As I'm sure the boys have told you, they were a bit ambitious when they made certain promises to you. But I assure you, the new lease agreement I've had them draw up is still quite favorable."

"Actually, Father, she's not here to sign an agreement with CHI." Christopher slides a stack of papers across the table toward Cyrus.

Cyrus's smile falters as he glances down at the paperwork. "I'm disappointed to hear that. Nevertheless, we have a list of potential tenants eager to rent from us."

"You misunderstand," Jason says. "Free and the other tenants will be signing a contract, but not with CHI."

Cyrus knits his brow, and Jason continues. "Bellamy Brothers Holdings is now the owner of the properties in question. In addition, there are a dozen other properties in Pointe Hill and surrounding neighborhoods we plan on investing in."

"I didn't authorize—"

"We don't need your authorization," Jason says. He glances at Christopher before returning his attention to Cyrus. "CHI won't be handling this or any other project in this market." He nods toward the contract Cyrus is holding. "Chronus Holding Incorporated has agreed to sell off its assets here, and turn over its existing local contracts to Bellamy Brothers, a company whose mission and goals more closely align with those of its owners and this community."

Cyrus drags his eyes from his eldest son and looks at the paperwork. His laugh is a quick, fierce bark. "And what makes you think I'd agree to any of this?"

Jason reaches for the office phone next to him and presses a button, "Melissa, please bring her in."

A few seconds later, Melissa opens the door. Her eyes are red rimmed, and unlike before, she makes no effort to make eye contact with the older Eubanks. Jessica walks through the door looking as impeccable as ever.

Cyrus rises in his chair. "Jessica, I thought you had already headed back to London," he says, his light tone carrying a slight edge.

Jessica takes the empty seat next to Christopher, and for a split second my heart races, but then, to my surprise, Jessica smiles at me.

Christopher clears his throat and when Cyrus turns his gaze toward him, Christopher says, "You will agree to this, because the alternative would end any political aspirations you may still have, and leave CHI with a public relations nightmare on its hands."

Cyrus's Adam's apple bobs, and for the first time since he's entered the room, I sense his anger simmering below the surface. He glances quickly at Jessica and then back at Christopher. "Son, I realize seeing Jessica and Shayne here was a surprise, but I still think there's a chance for the two of you to reconcile if only—"

"You'd be okay with your son reconciling with a woman you preyed on?"

Cyrus's eyes dart to Jessica. He creases his brow, and his face turns beet red. "You bitch," he hisses.

Christopher is out of his chair in a flash, reaching across the table, grabbing for his father's tie. "She was seventeen years old! You used her, just like you use everybody in your life."

Cyrus scoots back from the table just in time to avoid Christopher's grasp. "She seduced me," he whines like a petulant child. "Tell them! Tell them how you came to my office time and time again, pushing and pushing me, no matter how many times I refused."

"I was a teenager!" Jessica yells. "I craved the attention you paid me. The gifts, the dinners. And you swore me to secrecy, told me my father would be disgusted with me. That he would blame me for all of it. And I believed you. I was young and confused, and you took advantage of that."

"You were seventeen. Fully legal," he sputters, pointing a finger at her.

"But our mother wasn't, was she?" Jason asks, sliding a sheet of paper across the desk.

Cyrus leans over and looks at the document, and his face drains of all color.

"That is a copy of my birth certificate. We always knew Mom was a lot younger than you, but she would never tell us her age. I always thought it was vanity, but she was protecting you, wasn't she?" Jason says.

Cyrus stares at the document.

"She was seventeen when she had me. That means she was sixteen when she got pregnant, and she told me she'd been with you for about a year before she got pregnant."

Cyrus slumps in the chair. "She told me she was eighteen. Your mother looked and acted like someone much older." When neither of his sons speaks, Cyrus sighs. "What do you want?"

"It's all right there," Christopher says, pointing at the papers on the desk. "You allow us out of our contract with CHI. Allow us to take any clients that want to come with us. You agree to turn over business in Pointe Hill and neighboring towns. You keep all the properties up north and abroad. But we operate our new offices out of this building, and you raise no opposition to us being in this area."

"It's not that easy, we—"

"Make it easy," Jessica says with such force, Cyrus stops in his tracks. "I'm sure their mother wasn't your first victim, just as I'm certain I'm not the last. Make it easy, or I'll make things very hard for you."

Cyrus looks around the room then grabs the paperwork and stands. A cold smile stretches across his face. "I'll sign these. But if you think by any stretch of the imagination this is over, you've forgotten who taught you how to negotiate. Boys, you've won this battle, but I guarantee you, you won't win the war."

Cyrus stalks to the door and throws it open. It bangs against the wall as he storms down the hallway.

Christopher lays a comforting hand on Jessica's shoulder as she blots her eyes. I watch them, thinking about the bond they share, the bond they'll always share because of Shayne.

"Are you sure it was a good idea not telling him about Shayne?" Jason asks.

"He's the only innocent one in all of this," Jessica answers. "We might have to tell Cyrus one day, but not until we've decided Shayne is ready to hear it. And not until we're prepared to deal with whatever fallout comes our way. Speaking of Shayne, I've got to go pick him up from the sitter."

Jessica stands and tucks her purse under her arm. She heads toward the door, but stops just before leaving. "I realize this is something none of you asked for. Making an enemy out of Cyrus is a risk, one none of you would have had to take had I not lied. I'm sorry."

When she leaves, Jason clears his throat. "Jessica isn't exaggerating. We're now enemy number one with Cyrus. We need to prepare for when, not if, he decides to come at us." Jason pushes back from the table then nods before leaving Christopher and me alone in the room.

"Are you okay?" I ask him.

"I will be," he says, sighing heavily.

I walk over to where he's seated, and lean against the table next to him. He takes my hand. "Thank you. For being here, for supporting me."

A week ago, I called Carmen Holmes and told her I would be staying in Pointe Hill. My happy was taking shape, and that shape was filled with Cecelia's, and my mom, with Iris, and Anthony, and yes, Christopher. We were taking our time with our relationship, but he'd decided to stay in Pointe Hill, too, with his son by his side. And to make sure Shayne had both his father and mother in his life, Jessica would be staying in Pointe Hill and working for the newly formed Bellamy Brothers company.

He stands and kisses me. "And thanks for understanding about Jessica needing to be here with Shayne. Despite everything she did, she's not all bad, you know."

"I know. That's what I'm afraid of."

He cocks a brow.

"All bad is easy to hate. It's the in between that's hard. What Cyrus did to her was unforgiveable," I shake my head. "It doesn't excuse how she treated me, but I get it."

He pulls me into a long, lingering kiss that would go further except I remember we're in a conference room. "I should head back to the restaurant," I say when I pull away from him.

"We still on for later?"

"Definitely." I give him a peck on the cheek and head out.

In the lobby, I wave at Sam on my way out. "Coming by for lunch later, right? Mom's made black cake for dessert this week."

Sam rubs his stomach good-naturedly. "That's my favorite."

"Why do you think she made it?" I say, winking at him as I head out of the building.

THE BREAKFAST CROWD IS SLOWLY DWINDLING BY THE time I get back to the restaurant. Since the event, business has picked up so much that we've hired another server up front.

When I enter the kitchen, Anthony, Cassie, and Mom stop talking and turn to me. Christopher swore me to secrecy about Cyrus being Shayne's biological father, but they all know about Jason and Christopher's efforts to leave CHI and establish a new business, and they're all waiting to hear how things went.

"Well?" Mom asks, wiping her hands on a towel and walking up to me.

"He's going to sign. They gave him no choice, really. We're good for the foreseeable future. They'll institute a freeze on rent hikes, try to get some grant funding, and continue to support the mentor project."

Anthony lets out a whoop, and my mom claps her hands gleefully. "Thank God."

Cassie's reaction, however, is much more subdued.

"This is *good* news, Cassie," I say, giving her shoulders a squeeze.

She slips out of my grasp and returns to the prep work she was doing. "Does that mean you're not going to take that job in DC?" she asks.

"It's a great opportunity, but Pointe Hill is home. Cecelia's is home."

Cassie slams the knife she's using on the counter. "You're going to ruin this," she says, backing away from me. "You've just been lucky. Lucky people loved your dad so much they'll stick around for you. Lucky you're able to reproduce his recipes, but you're clueless about how to make the place grow."

"What are you talking about?" Anthony asks, coming to stand beside me.

"You're so enamored with your precious Free, you don't even see it, Anthony. So she got her boyfriend to waive off the rent hike for a few months. So what? Simone was right about this place. It will never make it the way it is now. Mr. Spalding saw that. He knew it was time for a change. And if he were alive, he'd want me to be the one making that change."

"Cassandra Miller," my mom warns. "Ray never wanted that. He always wanted Free to have this restaurant."

"But *I* was the one who stayed here and helped you guys when Free left. I was the one who came in early and left late, helping you get all those catering orders. And then *she* comes back in town, and it's like nothing I did even mattered." Cassie's eyes are watering and she's sniffling.

"Cassie, I appreciate everything you did to help me when I returned. I'm sorry if I didn't show it."

But Cassie continues as if she hasn't even heard me.

"How many times did I beg you to try my recipes? How many times? And then you go to one event and they ask you to lead the committee. Do you know how many of those chamber meetings I went to? I could barely ever get a chance to speak to them about my ideas for the Old Sixth Ward. For God's sake, you had an affair with a married man with three kids and they barely batted an eye."

I take a step back. "How did you know he had three kids, Cass? That wasn't anywhere in the blog post. I didn't even know he had children until he wrote me that—" I stop, everything suddenly becoming clear. "The letter Bryan wrote me. It was in my desk. You read it, didn't you?"

"Cassie, is that true?" Mom asks.

"I don't get it. Why is everyone always coming to your defense? What do you have that I don't?"

"You read the letter, then you told the reporter," I say, shaking my head in disbelief.

"And you made us think Danielle did it?" Anthony runs his hands over his face.

Cassie wipes her eyes and straightens her back. "Danielle is a trust-fund kid who's rebelling against her parents by dating the local foster-kid-done-good. Your hearing impairment is just icing on the cake."

"That's enough!" Mom yells, grabbing Cassie by the arm. "You apologize this minute."

Cassie shakes her head. "You're all unbelievable. I'm over this place. Over all of you. There's a bunch of competition coming to Pointe Hill and I won't be left behind. I'll go somewhere I'm appreciated." Cassie whips her apron over her head then blasts through the swinging doors, my mom trailing on her heels and Anthony close behind.

I watch the swinging door slowly come to a stop,

wondering how I missed the signs. Wondering what I could have done differently to change how Cassie felt. But I realize I'm no longer willing to sacrifice my happiness to please someone else. No longer willing to deny what I really want because of some ideal I've created in my head.

The pot on the stove pops, and I realize Mom left a batch of plantains frying. The sweet aroma floods the kitchen, and I run over and begin turning the oval slices. The bottoms are slightly burned, and this time, instead of chastising myself, I remind myself I'm not going to get them right every time, and that's okay.

CHAPTER THIRTY-FOUR

"Are you sure this is the address he gave you?" I ask Derrick as I step out of the car and study the large, sprawling structure.

"Yup," he says showing me the GPS address on his cell phone.

"Huh," I say, as Derrick waves goodbye and drives off, leaving me standing on the sidewalk in front of Pointe Hill High. I smooth down the maxi dress Iris bought me as a gift and insisted I wear tonight. The cerulean-blue print, with gold and black accents and jewel neckline, felt like overkill while I was getting dressed, but as I stand at the bottom of the long stairway leading into the building, I begin to suspect Iris knows more about tonight than she's let on.

Once inside, I'm immediately hit by a combination of smells—cafeteria food, bleached floors, and teen angst. The hallway looks shorter than I remember, but the large, gray tiles are as worn and shiny as the last time I walked on them. Everything seems smaller and less daunting than it did years ago, and that realization brings conflicting emotions of sadness and relief. Sadness because I let my time here shape so much of my life, and relief because after seven years, I'm finally moving forward.

A sandwich board sits on the floor at the end of the hallway. I trail my fingers along the lockers as I walk toward it. The large red arrow printed on the board points me down another hallway, and at the end of that hallway, a second sandwich board leads me to the gym's entrance.

I stop in front of the closed double doors and take a deep breath, pressing my forehead against the doorframe. The last time I was here, my heart was broken into a million pieces. My instinct is to flee, just as I did so many years ago. To run out of the building and keep running, leaving this part of my past in the past. But I'm tired of running. Tired of running from things said and unsaid, tired of being ashamed of who I was and all the things that happened back then. So I take a deep breath, push the doors open, and step into my past. Literally.

The gym is decorated almost exactly as it was on prom night. The walls are covered with purple and silver streamers. A disco ball hangs from the ceiling and twirls slowly, reflecting miniature rainbows across the room. Music plays from a pair of speakers on the bleachers, and silver and purple balloon arches mark a path to a single table set up in the center of the gym. Christopher waits for me at the table. Tears well in my eyes, and I swallow and take long, deep breaths to keep them from falling.

Christopher is wearing a tuxedo. His cummerbund and tie are cerulean blue and match my dress perfectly, confirming my suspicion that Iris had a hand in helping Christopher pull this off. My heart feels like it's going to burst, and I press a hand against my chest to try to steady myself. I open my mouth to speak, but let out a sob instead.

Christopher rushes forward and takes my hand in his.

"You told me you didn't know how to move forward, how to stay in Pointe Hill and be with me without bringing the pain from the past with us. I can't change what happened back then, Free, but I can help us make new memories." He looks around the gym. "When you think back on Pointe Hill High, I want you to remember *this* night. I want you to remember that you were and always will be the most brilliant, most beautiful woman in the room."

He pulls a small jewelry box from his pocket. "I was going to give this to you the morning of the District event, but I never got the chance to."

He opens the box and reveals a necklace, an exact replica of the one he'd given me so many years ago.

"How did you find it?" I manage between sobs.

"I had it made. And this time it's real," he says, smiling. "Read what it says inside."

I pull the necklace from the box and open the locket. The inscription is tiny, but I can make it out.

I'll catch you if you fall.

My hands are shaking as I hand the necklace to him and turn so he can put it on me. When he's done, he kisses me on the side of the neck, then turns me so I'm facing him. "You made that promise to me back when I had nothing. Now I'm making it to you. I'm here, Free. And I'm never leaving you again."

I open my mouth to speak, but Christopher raises a hand and stops me. "Please, let me get this all out while I have the nerve. Jason asked me to come back to Pointe Hill, but you're the reason I stayed. Before I came back, there was a space in here," he taps his chest, "that has been empty ever since that night I watched you run out of this gym. But these past few weeks you've begun to fill that space again. I still love you. I've *only* ever loved you. I know things won't always be easy. I know after all this time we will have to learn how to be together again, but tell me it's not too late for us. Tell me you still love me."

The tears are flowing freely now, mine and his, and I wrap my arms around him and pull him close. "I do love you, Christopher. I did then, and I do now."

He presses his forehead against mine and we sway slowly, in the middle of the gym. We dance past the memories of the first prom night, past the failed relationships, past the secrets and the lies. We dance past the seven years of being apart, and the past few months of learning how to be together.

"I know what it looks like now," I say quietly.

"What, what looks like?" Christopher asks, pulling me tighter.

"The shape of my happy," I answer, sighing and leaning as far into Christopher as I can, knowing he'll catch me if I fall.

EPILOGUE

SPRING

From across the crowded restaurant, Christopher catches my attention. The Tuckers have been talking to him nonstop for the past fifteen minutes, but his focus is on me. He raises his glass and smiles. My fingers instinctively reach up to the locket around my neck.

The party was my idea. A last-minute send off for Mom, who is headed to Paris with Sam for three weeks. Although she's made a point of mentioning they'd be staying with Sam's sister, who has several bedrooms.

I scan the room, full to overflowing with friends and neighbors. Kids running between their parents' legs, teenagers huddled in corners. Anthony and Danielle are talking at the far end of the front counter. I'm not sure Danielle has forgiven Anthony for not believing her, but I think she's trying.

Jason and Iris are behind the counter, serving scoops of ice cream the Fosters brought over, and if the looks they're exchanging are any indication, there's much more going on between them than they're letting on.

Shayne runs over to Christopher and he crouches and studies what his son has brought to show him.

"They look so much alike, don't they?" Jessica's sudden appearance disarms me, and my hand jerks a little, spilling bright red drops of sorrel out of my glass and onto the tile floor. She's standing close enough that I smell the subtle fragrance of her flowery perfume. "Thank you, Free," she says.

I glance at her. "For what?"

"For being so understanding about me and Shayne always being a part of Christopher's life. It can't be easy for you knowing how much time we spend together." There's a smile on her face, but her eyes offer a challenge.

I run my fingers across the locket and look at Christopher and Shayne. "I know we've had our issues in the past, Jessica, but I'm hoping for Shayne's sake, we can move beyond them and figure out a way to make this work."

Shayne runs off to play with a group of children, and Christopher straightens. He wears his hair a little shorter now, so the gray patch shows clearly. He's dressed casually tonight, in a plain T-shirt and a pair of jeans that rest low on his hips. His smile is mischievous and focused only on me.

"It can't be easy on you, either," I say, thrusting my glass into Jessica's hand. "Knowing that *that* man right there comes home to me every night must just kill you."

I walk across the room, wishing I had eyes on the back of my head to see Jessica's reaction when I pull Christopher toward me and kiss him.

"What was that for?" he asks, making a satisfied sound.

"Just reminding someone who needs a little reminding."

I give him a quick peck and grab his glass. "Everyone, can I have your attention please." The room quiets as conversations stop and all eyes turn to me. "Last year was challenging for us. We lost Daddy, then we almost lost this place. But during that trying period, I was reminded of a few things." I turn to Mom, Iris, and Anthony. "I was reminded that family is there for each other, especially when things get hard." To Christopher, I say, "I learned that though we can't change the past, we can change the way we remember it and the power we allow it to have over our lives. And I was reminded why this place will always be my home. To Cecelia's," I say, raising my glass.

"To Cecelia's!" the room lets out in a cheer.

I look up at the wall behind the counter. We've moved my grandmother's picture to the front of the restaurant. On the left of it is a picture of Daddy, wearing his old apron, and on the right, a picture of Mom and me in the kitchen.

Later, I see Mom standing alone at the front door. She motions me over, opening the door then leading me outside. Dusk is settling over Pointe Hill. The dogwood tree at the edge of the sidewalk has shed most of its delicate white leaves, creating a sort of welcome mat at the restaurant's front door.

Mom and I walk to the edge of the sidewalk. She tucks a braid back into my bun then threads her arm through mine as we look up at Cecelia's new awning. It fits perfectly with the row of awnings and white-washed brick storefronts that now line the street.

"You think Daddy's seeing all of this, Mom?"

"I know he is."

"You think he's happy?"
"Are you happy, Free?"
"I am."
"Then your Dad is happy, and so am I."

THE END

MORE POINTE HILL DRAMA

I hope you enjoyed reading *Free Falling* as much as I enjoyed writing it. I love Pointe Hill and the people in it, and I'm working to bring you more stories in the series, starting with Free's feisty and headstrong cousin, Iris Hauss. Iris has her own secrets, and they're threatening to reveal themselves at the worst possible time. I think you'll love Iris, and I can't wait to share her story with you.

In the meantime, if you don't already have access to the latest about what's happening in Pointe Hill, visit me on the web at www.ggwynter.com.

IF YOU ENJOYED THIS BOOK,
PLEASE SPREAD THE LOVE!

Word of mouth and honest reviews left on retail sites are the best ways to let other readers know you've discovered a book you like. If you've enjoyed this book please consider leaving a review—as short or long as you like—wherever you purchased your copy.

Thank you very much.

ABOUT THE AUTHOR

G.G. Wynter is the author of *Free Falling*, a 2016 Georgia Romance Writers' Maggie Award finalist and a 2017 Kayak Author Award finalist. When she's not traveling between the Marvel and DC Universes, you can find her online at www.ggwynter.com, on Instagram at @ggwynterwrites, on Facebook at @ggwynter, and on Twitter @ggwynterwrites. You can also email her at connect@ggwynter.com. She'd love to hear from you!

www.ingramcontent.com/pod-product-compliance
Lightning Source LLC
Chambersburg PA
CBHW021006120726
47905CB00009B/2887